RUDE AWAKENING

Cody's eyes blinked open. Morning light, white and harsh, glared through an open window. He blinked again.

Something hard and cold nudged his left shoulder. He moaned; it prodded him again.

"Wha—?" Biting off his words, he came awake. He was staring directly into the dark muzzle of a pistol.

Slowly, cautiously, he lifted his gaze above the well of blue-black steel pointed between his eyes.

"Charity Quitman."

"Didn't know if you'd remember me or not." A dry sound something like a chuckle pushed from her throat. "Now, I'd like to introduce Mr. Samuel Colt.

"Actually, Mr. Colt and I have known each other for years," Cody said.

"Good. Then you're aware that I can take off the top of your skull with one shot from this."

The threat sounded deadly cold. Cody nodded.

"I also want you to know that that's what I'll do, if you don't do exactly what I say." She pressed the muzzle against his forehead to emphasize her point. . . .

Cody's Law

Ask your bookseller for the books you have missed

CODY'S LAW
Book 7

END OF
THE LINE

Matthew S. Hart

 Producers of **The Holts, The Patriots, and The Frontier Trilogy: Westward!**

Book Creations Inc., Canaan, NY • *Lyle Kenyon Engel, Founder*

BANTAM BOOKS
NEW YORK • TORONTO • LONDON • SYDNEY • AUCKLAND

END OF THE LINE

*A Bantam Book / published by arrangement with
Book Creations Inc.*

Bantam edition / November 1992

*Produced by Book Creations Inc.
Lyle Kenyon Engel, Founder*

ISBN 0-553-29764-3

Published simultaneously in the United States and Canada

Bantam Books are published by Bantam Books, a division of Bantam Doubleday
Dell Publishing Group, Inc. Its trademark, consisting of the words "Bantam Books"
and the portrayal of a rooster, is Registered in U.S. Patent and Trademark Office
and in other countries. Marca Registrada. Bantam Books, 666 Fifth Avenue, New
York, New York 10103.

PRINTED IN THE UNITED STATES OF AMERICA

RAD   0   9   8   7   6   5   4   3   2   1

CHAPTER
1

As Sam Cody climbed the stairs to the second floor of the Jefferson Hotel, his right hand casually dipped into the pocket of his jacket and gripped the butt of the .38-caliber Remington nestled there. Pointing the revolver ahead of him, he lightly rested his forefinger over the trigger, ready to fire through the pocket if necessary.

The pistol, an inch sawed off its barrel, felt awkward and light in a hand accustomed to the heft of a Frontier Colt, but it snuggled tidily into the pocket of the constricting brown suit that the Texas Ranger wore. The dandyish clothing on his tall, sinewy frame and the brown derby perched atop his head were as alien to his body as the six-shooter was to his hand. Though in his early thirties, Cody could count the number of times he had worn a suit on the fingers of one hand—without using all of them up.

Pausing at the head of the stairs, he glanced to the right down an L-shaped hallway, then peered straight ahead. A black-suited gentleman with muttonchop sideburns stopped before a room at the end of the hall, unlocked the door, then disappeared inside. Cody heard the faint click of the lock returning to its niche as the man secured the door from within. The man was just another of the hotel's occupants.

Cody sighed inaudibly, then glanced over a shoulder and nodded to the man and woman waiting at the foot of the stairs, signaling that the way was clear. But the big Ranger's right hand remained around the pistol in his pocket—just in case.

He was overreacting, he chided himself. But then, playing bodyguard to one of the nation's biggest railroad moguls wasn't exactly his forte. Renegade Indians, border *bandidos*, and cattle rustlers were far more suited to his tastes and abilities.

But when a man was a Ranger, that man did what his superiors ordered.

Major John B. Jones, commander of the Frontier Battalion, which included Cody's own Company C headquartered in Del Rio, had assigned Cody as one of two bodyguards to Jay Gould and his wife during their stay in Jefferson, Texas. So for the past five days Cody had been a bodyguard, along with fellow Ranger Aaron Hayden, who hailed from San Antonio.

Gould and his wife climbed within three steps of the Ranger, who then turned to his right and walked ahead of the couple as they moved down the hallway. Cody paused again when he reached a left-hand turn in the hall and glanced around the corner to see Hayden standing outside the door to the Goulds' room. Hayden nodded that all was fine.

Cody turned to the couple. "Mr. and Mrs. Gould, the way is clear. Have a restful night."

Neither the short, full-bearded Gould nor his petite wife replied as they walked past Cody toward Hayden, who unlocked their room for them.

Cody idly tugged at his thick, dark mustache while he watched the man and woman saunter down the hall. Maybe he *wasn't* overreacting. If Jay Gould evoked the same dislike in other men that he stirred in Cody, it was easy to understand somebody deciding to take a shot at him. The man seemed to compensate for his five-foot-two height with at least a rod of arrogance. If there was one thing Texans didn't tolerate, it was a man who set himself above others. And as a native son of the Lone Star State, the ways of Texans were something Cody personally knew.

Gould had come here amid the East Texas piney woods to convince the Jefferson city fathers that it'd be economically advantageous for them to allow his Texas and Pacific Railroad to pass through this, Texas's largest city, as the railway sought to connect the expanding frontier with the eastern states.

Of course, having Texas's booming trade center placed on the railroad line didn't come without a price, and that was the hitch as far as Jefferson's city elders were concerned. Gould demanded free land to lay his railroad tracks on as well as land within the city itself for his enterprise.

Unlike the majority of the vast lands west of the Mississippi River, Texas had been an independent republic before joining the United States. That meant there was no free government land to give railroad developers as an incentive for the construction of new lines. Gould had spent the last week in one meeting after another with Jefferson's officials and prominent businessmen, attempting to convince them that the price he asked would seem like a mere drop in the bucket when compared to the prosperity the railroad would bring to Jefferson.

How Gould had fared Cody could only guess. He wasn't privy to what occurred in those meetings, just stood outside closed doors like some damn sentry making certain that only those with the proper password were allowed to pass.

"They're all mine for the night, Cody," Aaron Hayden said as he locked the hotel room behind the Goulds.

Cody released the Remington, slipped his right hand from his pocket, and sketched a casual salute at Hayden. "I'll check back with you before I turn in," he said. "Right now I want to find something to eat. I haven't had a bite since breakfast."

When Hayden waved him on his way, Cody retraced his steps along the hotel hallway and down the stairs into a lobby spacious even by Texas standards. Despite now being officially off duty, his gaze automatically darted around the room. But except for two women deep in conversation on a sofa to his left and a young clerk behind the desk, the lobby was empty. Cody walked to the double-doored entrance and stepped into the warm, sticky humidity of an East Texas summer night.

The shriek of a steam whistle sliced through air. Looking in its direction, Cody could make out the ghostly form of a whitewashed riverboat alongside Jefferson's wharves two blocks from the hotel. For a long moment the craft appeared to lie dead in the water as the stern-wheeler reversed its churning; then the boat swung northward to move downstream and be swallowed by the darkness.

Cody studied the ten other paddle wheelers lining Jefferson's docks. There stood Gould's greatest opposition in the city, the Ranger mused. Steel rails and steam locomotives catered to America's love of speed, but railroads were expensive for passengers and cargo. Riverboats could still move both, though at a far more leisurely pace, for mere pennies a mile.

Jefferson had sprung up on the banks of Big Cypress Creek, one of Texas's few navigable waterways. Thanks to a massive, two-hundred-mile-long logjam on the Red River, an obstruction whose existence was known since the first Europeans had discovered the river a couple of centuries earlier, water spilled from the Red into swampy Caddo Lake and then into the Cypress, swelling the creek into a full-fledged river. It was via the Cypress and Caddo Lake that riverboats gained access to the waterways of Louisiana. Cotton and riverboats had produced this prosperous city of fifteen thousand that not even the Civil War had diminished.

Turning from the riverboats, Cody walked toward a saloon down the street, thinking as he went that, if anything, the war had helped establish Jefferson as Texas's dominant commercial center, shipping tons of salted beef as well as gunpowder that had been manufactured here to the Confederate forces. Both had been unpluckable thorns in the Union's side. During the war, Cody remembered reading about a failed blue-coat mission to destroy the gunpowder plant.

Entering the saloon, Cody found an empty table near the bar, hailed a passing waiter, and was informed that the fare for the evening meal was fried catfish, new potatoes and green beans, and corn bread. The Ranger gave a crooked grin. "Then I guess I'll have the catfish. Oh, and bring a beer now and a fresh one with my meal."

The waiter hurried off, then quickly returned with a mug of cold beer. Sipping it with satisfaction, Cody looked around the saloon. Friday night had brought an increase in business compared to the other nights he had visited the place. At least a hundred men sat crowded about tables or stood elbow to elbow along the bar. Most had the look of farmers come to the big city to celebrate the weekend.

Now and then Cody caught a glimpse of a barmaid leading one of the patrons up a flight of wooden stairs at the back of the saloon to disappear behind one of the five doors at the top of the landing. On another night he might have been tempted to take the trip up those stairs himself to sample the pleasures to be found behind those doors, but tonight the rumbling of his stomach took precedence over the desire of another portion of his anatomy.

And speaking of his anatomy . . . Cody's right hand crept toward the stiff, starched collar of the white dress shirt biting at his neck. He willed the hand back to the table before his fingers loosened the tie, which felt like a noose around his neck, and popped open the collar studs. As long as he was in Jefferson, he wasn't Samuel Clayton Woodbine Cody, but Sam Cass, railroad agent.

Disgust curled Cody's mouth. He was something of a lone wolf and used to undercover assignments from Captain Wallace Vickery, who commanded Ranger Company C. But this assignment bordered on being ridiculous. Here he was, a badge-wearing Texas Ranger, playacting the role of another kind of lawman—or an *almost* lawman, since railroad agents weren't peace officers under the Texas Constitution.

For the second time in as many minutes he quelled the nagging urge to rip away the tie and open the collar. Or even better, return to his hotel room and change into the familiar comfort of the blue work shirt and denim pants he normally wore. Of equal pleasure would be the familiar feel of his high-topped boots and well-worn Stetson. The ugly brown shoes laced to his feet cramped his toes until they felt as though they were going to knot one on top of the other. And as for the damn derby perched on his head . . . Well, he just gave silent thanks that his fellow Rangers back in Del Rio couldn't see him now.

The only good thing Cody could think of when it came to

the monkey suit he wore was that he hadn't shelled out good money to buy it. Clothes, food, weapons, horses, and tack were usually out-of-pocket expenses for a Texas Ranger. But the taxpayers of the state of Texas had footed the bill for these duds. An amused smile replaced Cody's scowl. Half of those taxpayers would no doubt agree with him that their money had been misappropriated.

The distinctive sound of shuffling cards drew his attention to a table in the middle of the room, where a man in a green-checkered suit and brown derby dealt five cards to each of his five companions at the table. Cody smiled. Five-card draw. Now *there* was a gentlemanly pastime worthy of pursuing on a Friday night—and one he would attend after his meal. That was, if either of the two empty chairs at the table remained vacant.

The waiter returned, bringing Cody's second beer along with a plate piled with a couple of one-pound catfish and a small mountain of new potatoes and green beans as well as rings from a fresh-cut onion. Draining the last swallow of the first beer, Cody attacked the meal.

The picked bones of one of the catfish lay to one side of the plate before he took a small breather and glanced over at the poker table. The two vacant chairs had stayed empty.

A steamboat whistle screamed in the distance, and as Cody returned to his meal, thoughts of Gould, railroads, and river-boats edged aside images of a royal flush. When given this assignment, he had boned up on the recent history of both Jefferson and the railroads, learning that after the Civil War the rails had stolen away the beef trade, but even that hadn't affected the city's economy. In fertile, rain-rich East Texas, cotton remained king. Transporting bales of cotton was still the domain of riverboats and sailing ships. Gould had his work cut out for him, Cody thought, in trying to convince Jefferson that a railroad would improve the life that flourished here.

And Gould wasn't the most reputable railroad man Cody had ever had the pleasure to meet. The Ranger couldn't blame Jefferson's businessmen for the leery arch of their eyebrows that he had noticed more than once. Back East, Gould had inflated the price of Erie Line stock until it was all but valueless, creating a scandal as well as court litigation when the railroad was sold for $5 million. Worse, to Cody's way of thinking, was Gould's scheme to corner the gold market in '69. The result was one of the worst panics in American financial history when the bottom suddenly dropped out and gold prices plummeted. Black Friday was the name the newspapers had given to that infamous day.

And now Major Jones had assigned Cody to wet-nurse such a man.

The thought was more than a little disgusting to the Ranger. Worse, he had been pulled from a two-week-long chase across half of Texas, taking him from El Paso to San Antonio, that would have resulted in the arrest of the Mexican rustler Diego Alvarez. Would have, Cody thought angrily, had Major Jones not yanked him off Alvarez's trail to guard Gould during his Jefferson trip.

A week had passed since Cody had traveled deep into the piney woods of East Texas. Diego Alvarez and two hundred head of rustled prime beef on the hoof seemed so distant now. In truth, the Ranger would have taken no pleasure in bringing Alvarez in. On more than one occasion the Mexican bandit had saved his hide—risking his own in the process. Cody admitted to himself that the man was downright likable ... except for his downright annoying habit of conducting all his business outside the law.

Alvarez would have to wait, whether Cody liked it or not. For the time being he was stuck in Jefferson, making certain no one decided to take a potshot at Jay Gould until the man's business in the port city was complete.

And there had been threats to Gould's life, at least three of them. Major Jones had shown three anonymous letters to Cody in San Antonio. Whether the threats were real or merely a ruse by riverboat owners to frighten Gould and keep him out of Jefferson, Cody couldn't say—and Jones couldn't either. The simple fact of the matter was that Gould had shown the letters to the governor, who in turn had passed them to Jones, along with the request that two Rangers be assigned to Gould during his stay in the East Texas city.

Jones had determined that those two Rangers should go undercover. The major wanted the railroad mogul guarded but didn't want to attract unnecessary attention to him. Two Rangers with badges pinned to their chests would draw the eye of every man, woman, and child in Jefferson, a city that prided itself on its law officers and their ability to handle whatever problems arose.

And without a doubt, Cody was certain, an unspoken reason the governor had requested two Rangers to the simple task of guarding Jay Gould was to keep close tabs on the man's activities. The Erie stock scandal and Black Friday would assure Gould's close scrutiny by those in power in the state capitol. A man who had rocked, if not cracked, the financial foundation of the whole country demanded such attention. Especially in Texas, Cody considered, which was still trying to get its financial feet firmly under it after the long, hard years of Reconstruction.

The crisp, alluring sound of cards being shuffled wedged its way into Cody's reflections. Protecting Jay Gould and his wife had occupied his every waking moment since arriving in Jefferson. Tonight Cody was determined to reward his sustained vigilance with a few hours of relaxation.

And perhaps even a little profit, he thought, a hint of a smile quirking his mouth.

Slipping a hand into the left pocket of his brown trousers, he withdrew a small roll of bills and counted the greenbacks. Forty dollars. More than enough for a stake in a friendly game. If the pots required greater resources, he had no business sitting down at the table.

Draining the last of his beer, Cody waved the waiter over. He ordered a third round, then requested, "Please inquire at that table if those two empty seats are reserved or open." He tilted his head toward the poker game.

The waiter glanced over at the players, then told Cody, "Doc Pruitt and Harvey Caldwell usually sit in on Sheriff Howell's Friday-night game. My bet's them chairs are open to whoever's got the spirit, since Doc and Harv're down in Austin. But I'll check it out with the sheriff for you, if you're a-mind.''

''I'm a-mind,'' Cody confirmed with a nod.

Rather than going to the bar for the ordered beer, the waiter first walked over to the poker table and bent to whisper into the ear of a man with his back to Cody. When the waiter straightened, the seated man shifted in his chair and glanced over his shoulder, seeking out Cody. The man's dark-eyed gaze found Cody, who nodded, and the sheriff then nodded to the waiter, who stepped back across the room.

''Sheriff Howell says them chairs are open to all comers,'' the waiter announced.

Asking that his beer be brought to the game table, Cody got up and crossed to the waiting players, taking the closest vacant chair. Sheriff Howell rose and stretched out a welcoming hand, and Cody guessed the sheriff to be a year or two younger than himself, in spite of the bushy mustache that drooped below the corners of the lawman's mouth. ''Name's Manly Howell, city sheriff here in Jefferson,'' the lawman said. ''I've seen you durin' the day with our city's distinguished visitor, Mr. Jay Gould. Work for Gould, do you?''

''Just while he's in town. Hired on as a bodyguard,'' Cody answered as he shook Howell's hand. ''My name's Sam Cass.''

The sheriff openly assessed Cody, as though by studying his external characteristics, he could gauge his internal character. The Ranger was well above average height, and his sinewy physique, which some called thin, was all muscle—a fact that anyone who challenged him didn't find out until sampling the lightning reflexes that guided solid fists. And while he could never be called handsome, his rugged, weathered face set many a female heart aflutter.

''Over here's Glevis Hudler''—Howell released Cody's hand and gestured to the man on his left—''town blacksmith. And this is . . .''

The introductions proceeded around the table. Besides Howell and Hudler, the remaining three players were Wade Moore, farmer; William Egger, cotton broker from New Orleans; and, in the green-checkered suit, Titus Newman, a traveling shoe salesman whom Cody had sat next to.

As Cody shook Newman's hand, Howell explained, "This is a friendly game. White chips'll cost you a nickel, red ones a dime, and blue two bits. And I'll warn you ahead of time, the cards've been kind to Newman there all evenin'. He's done taken twenty-five dollars off me."

Which was fifteen dollars over the point that he himself would call the game a bust and turn in for the night, Cody thought. He pulled twenty dollars from his pocket and exchanged it for ten dollars in chips and two fives.

"Ante's a nickel," Newman said. He tossed a white chip to the middle of the table and began to shuffle the cards. "The game's five-card draw. No wild cards, gentlemen."

Dropping a white chip at the center of the table, Cody waited for Newman to complete the deal before picking up his hand.

Rule one of a friendly game: Set a loss limit, and when it's reached, fold the cards and bid one's fellow players a good night. Cody broke that rule. Ten dollars had been his limit. He was twenty dollars in the hole when he reached into his pocket to buy another ten dollars' worth of chips.

Gambling fever hadn't seduced him. Of that he was certain. While he enjoyed a good poker game, he wasn't addicted to the gaming tables. But right now he was hooked. He had taken the bait, and now he was being reeled in, ready for the waiting net held out by an angler.

He wasn't the only fish at the table, either. Sheriff Howell's losses now totaled sixty dollars. The farmer was thirty in the hole and the blacksmith forty. The cotton broker fared no better than Howell, having also lost sixty dollars. When tallied together the losses didn't total a single pot of some of the games Cody had sat in. But for a friendly game that had begun as recreation, relaxation, and conversation, the money that had passed across the table had the smell of blood to it.

The man with his nostrils flared wide with that scent was the shoe salesman, Titus Newman—Newman in his outrageous green-checkered suit, looking more like a circus clown than a gambler.

Cody studied the man out of the corner of his eye as Newman shuffled and dealt five cards to those around the table. The salesman smiled when he lifted his hand and fanned it open.

Cody picked up his own hand and stared in the faces of three queens. Garbage stood beside the three ladies. His gaze shifted about the table, finally settling again on Newman.

It was Newman who had hooked Cody, and it was Newman who kept Cody betting long after he had exceeded his evening's limit. The man's luck was too uncanny to be explained by the fall of the pasteboards. His manipulation of the game went beyond the simple shuffle and dealing of the cards.

Yet Cody had watched him carefully for hours. Newman didn't deal from the bottom of the deck—or if he did, he did it so skillfully that it was undetectable. And the salesman hadn't marked the deck. On the few occasions that Cody had won the deal, his fingertips carefully explored the backs of the cards as well as their edges, searching for nicks, scratches, and creases. There was nothing.

Wade Moore began the betting with a quarter. Every man at the table saw the bet. Newman called for cards. Cody tossed in two and drew two others that did nothing to improve the power of his three queens.

Cody decided that the salesman had to be using a holdout. But where did Newman hide the device? Cody hadn't seen him going to his vest or coat. He had even brushed against the salesman's arm to see if his sleeves concealed a spring-loaded mechanism. Nothing—Cody neither saw nor felt anything. Yet . . .

The betting was fifty cents when it came around the table. Cody met the wager and raised it another quarter. Newman folded—an action Cody had come to expect. Like an angler who expertly reeled in the line then eased up to prevent it from snapping, Newman was smart enough to allow the others to win hands occasionally—hands with pots never amounting to more than five dollars. Newman knew how to dance a fly across the top of the water to bring the big fish up from the bottom.

Howell, Egger, and Moore called the bet. Cody placed his three queens on the table faceup. They beat Moore's pair of aces and Egger's duo of kings as well as the three nines Jefferson's sheriff tossed to the table.

Raking in the small pot, Cody added the chips to the three piles in front of him, then gathered the cards in a neat stack. If Newman employed a holdout, there was only one way to find out. Cody's thumbnail scratched two parallel lines down the bottom of the deck, marking them. He passed the cards to Howell for the cut, then dealt.

Newman's luck once again changed. He won the hand and regained control of the deal. Cody sat back and waited as the salesman won the next hand and then the next.

It was when Howell took the following hand that Cody acted. With a flick of the wrist, he sent his cards sailing across the table toward Howell. The hand, as Cody had planned, scattered in five different directions at once, two of the cards falling to the floor.

"Sorry," Cody apologized immediately. "I'll pick them up for you."

Before the sheriff could answer, Cody bent down, his gaze darting to Newman's legs in the hope of detecting the telltale bulge of a holdout. Nothing.

"Hell, let 'em be," Howell said. "It's time we had a new deck anyway. This one ain't doin' me no good."

Cody smiled slightly. That was exactly what he had wanted. If Newman was tucking away cards, those he now held were neatly marked.

The Ranger picked up the fallen cards, and as he straightened up, his smile widened. There beneath the table, positioned directly under Newman's right hand, was the holdout. The device was a simple clip made from a watch spring and tacked beneath the table. In the parlance of gamblers it was called a "bug," and the concept was so old-fashioned that it hadn't been employed since the heyday of riverboats on the Mississippi before the war.

And that was what had made the holdout so hard to find. Cody had expected a complicated mechanical contraption hidden within Newman's clothes, designed to feed winning cards down a sleeve. But using this bug meant that a cough, a twist in his chair, or taking a swig of beer was all Newman needed to distract watching eyes while his right fingers darted beneath the table to retrieve the waiting cards.

Of the cards held in the bug, Cody glimpsed only the face of a jack of spades before he sat upright again and passed the spilled hand to Howell. The sheriff added the cards to the deck he set aside, then opened another deck of blue-backed Riverboat Playing Cards. He shuffled and passed them for the cut before dealing.

Not one card in Cody's hand matched. It didn't matter. If he wanted to catch Newman with marked cards he had holed away, he had to make the salesman use those cards now. The only way to do that was to bait a hook of his own. When a four-bit bet came around the table, the Ranger raised it to a dollar. The remaining five players saw the raise. Howell asked for discards. Cody stood pat.

A flash in Newman's brown eyes when he glanced at Cody said that the salesman was ready to take the bait. Cody dropped four more blue chips into the pot to reopen the betting.

Newman met the dollar wager, then bumped it higher with two more blue chips. Sheriff Howell saw the bet. The rest of the players folded; a dollar fifty was far too rich for a game that was supposed to be no more than a few hands of friendly Friday-night poker.

Cody glanced back at the five mismatched cards in his hand. While the pot might be high enough to drive away the weak hands the others held, it might not be steep enough to assure that Newman employed the cards he had neatly hidden in the bug tacked beneath the table. Cody had to sweeten the bet to assure that the salesman dipped into his holdout cards. At the same time the Ranger had to be certain that when the showdown came, *he* was the one who called Newman's hand, forcing the man to lay his cards on the table.

He tossed another dollar in chips to the mounting pile.

Cody turned to the salesman. "I'll see you and raise another fifty cents."

Newman didn't hesitate. He matched the raise, then added a dollar of his own.

Howell shook his head when he dropped his cards facedown on the table. "You boys are gettin' too rich for my blood. Fight it out amongst yourselves."

Which was exactly what Cody wanted. He tossed in the needed dollar, then pushed in four more blue chips.

Newman smiled. "Mr. Cass, we might as well make this interesting, seeing as it's come down to you and me. I'll see that raise and up it five dollars."

The farmer gasped, and Sheriff Howell cleared his throat.

Cody kept his eyes on Newman—and saw what he wanted. The salesman bent slightly forward to edge the pile of blue chips into the pot with his left hand, and his right hand dropped below the edge of the table. Cody had no doubt that the salesman switched the cards in his hand with those in the holdout.

"You're called," Cody said, shoving five dollars to the center of the table. "Let's see what you're holding."

"Royal flush." Newman fanned his cards atop the table. "In spades."

"Interesting." Cody looked at Sheriff Howell. "Seems we have a little problem here."

The Ranger reached out and snatched up the undealt cards and spread them faceup on the table. He didn't have to describe what problem he meant. The faces of the spade royalty buried in the deck was all the explanation needed.

"What is this!" Newman sputtered with just the right amount of indignation. "What are you trying to pull?"

Keeping close watch on the salesman, Cody told Howell, "Sheriff, I've suspected that things have been less than aboveboard in this game for quite a while now. Before retiring that deck beside you, I marked the bottoms of the cards with two thumbnail scratches. . . .''

"I knew you were up to something!" Newman yelped, his indignation heightened to outrage. "This man's a self-proclaimed cheat! He should be run out of town on a rail! He should be taken and—''

"I believe that if you check Newman's flush," Cody said loudly enough to the sheriff to drown out the salesman's outburst, "you'll find his cards have marks that match. I also think you'll find that he has a bug tacked beneath the table where he kept—''

Newman's right hand dropped toward the bottom of his vest. Cody didn't need to see the weapon to know that the man had gone for a belly gun. Like an uncoiling spring Cody's left arm shot out, and his balled fist hammered solidly into Newman's throat, smashing into the Adam's apple.

A half-strangled moan sputtered from the salesman as the force of the blow sent him tumbling backward on his chair. A .44-caliber Colt revolver, its barrel sawed off to a mere inch, flew from his hand and careened across the saloon's wooden floor.

Cody's strategically aimed fist was meant to leave Newman incapacitated on the floor while Sheriff Howell decided the appropriate action to deal with the tinhorn. But though the blow did spill the salesman to the floor, he didn't remain there. Rolling from the overturned chair, he managed to right himself with surprising alacrity and came straight for Cody with outstretched hands.

Shoving from his own chair, Cody faced the charging man. Newman's fingers were inches from his throat when Cody sidestepped, leaving his left leg trailing behind him.

Newman hit the outstretched leg at a full run and went sprawling facedown on the floor. But his recovery came as quickly as his first rebound, and he scrambled to his feet and spun around to face Cody.

This time the Ranger was prepared. His right fist buried itself in Newman's stomach. The salesman groaned as his body doubled over. In an arching undercut, Cody's left fist lashed into Newman's exposed chin.

The salesman staggered back but managed to remain upright on teetering legs. His head jerked from side to side as though trying to shake off the punishing effects of the blows.

Which was the last thing Cody wanted.

Taking one quick step toward Newman, Cody again struck with his right fist. Again he connected with the salesman's chin, and this time the weight of his whole body was behind the blow.

There was no groan or moan. Newman swayed back and forth. Finally, like a felled loblolly pine, he dropped and crashed to the floor.

In a wide-legged stance, ready to meet a renewed attack, Cody stood over his opponent with raised fists. But Newman didn't move— not so much as a twitch.

"Two scratches are on his cards as well as the rest of the old deck, just like you said."

Cody blinked and looked up from the unconscious man. For the first time since Newman had attempted to pull his belly gun, Cody was aware of his surroundings. Half the saloon's patrons stood in a wide circle around him and the fallen salesman. Here and there men exchanged money, and Cody realized that the outcome of the fight had been the subject of wagering, as if he and Newman had been prizefighters in a ring.

"I had my suspicions that he was palmin' cards, but damned if I could catch him at it. Your eye was a mite sharper'n mine."

Cody turned toward the voice. Sheriff Manly Howell still sat at the table, one hand holding Newman's cards, the other the remainder of the old deck. The lawman studied the two thumbnail scratches a moment longer, then glanced up at Cody as though the barroom brawl had gone completely unnoticed. "Should've thought of this little trick myself." He shrugged.

"Wish you had," Cody answered. "I've no particular fondness for men throwing down on me."

"You say he had a holdout stashed under the table?" Howell asked, nodding toward Newman's chair with no outward show of concern for either Cody's or Newman's condition.

Cody reached beneath the table, pulled the bug free, and tossed it in front of the sheriff. "Had it tacked where he could get at it with his right hand when he leaned forward to drop a bet into the pot."

"Haven't seen one of these in years. Almost forgot what they looked like." Howell lifted the holdout and scrutinized it. He then turned to the other players at the table. "You boys tally up that pile of chips. See that we all get what we started the night with. What's left will be Newman's winnings. Divide it equally. We might as well get somethin' for our time."

"What about him?" Cody asked, glancing down at the un-conscious salesman. "Want me to help you drag him to a cell?"

The sheriff stuffed the bug into a pocket before he looked up at the Ranger and shook his head. "Jailin' a man like that'd be a waste of the taxpayers' money. I'd have to see he was fed three meals a day, and then there'd be the cost of a trial and all. Don't seem hardly worth it to me; does it to you?"

Cody squinted at the lawman in disbelief. "You don't in-tend to charge this man?"

Howell shook his head as he stood. "Got a better way of handlin' tinhorns here in Jefferson." He smiled at the other players. "You boys take our friend there over to Jay Til-den's—and the sooner the better. You might have your hands full if he wakes up on you. From the looks of it he's got more fight in him'n I imagined."

The sheriff's words surprised Cody; they were the first in-dication that the lawman had even noticed that there had been a fight.

"Who's this Jay Tilden?" he asked.

"Runs a dry-goods store out near the edge of town." How-ell watched as the men started to drag Newman from the sa-loon by his heels. "Jay keeps a good supply of tar and feathers laid in for such occasions as this. Care to come along and help me and the boys see that our friend there gets a proper treat-ment?"

Cody chuckled. Trials and judges might be what were called for in law books, but sometimes Texas's own brand of justice was a damned sight swifter and more appropriate.

"Think I'll pass this time. It's getting late, and I've got work in the morning."

Howell shrugged, hiked his eyebrows, and strode toward the saloon's batwings after his companions. He reached the swinging doors and turned back to Cody. "Markin' them cards was a sharp trick." His eyes challenged Cody's. "I hope you ain't in a habit of doin' such at the poker table. I'd feel down-right bad if I was forced to dress you up in a suit of tar and feathers before you left my city."

Cody grinned. "I rarely employ such tactics . . . and only under the most dire circumstances when there's a man wearing a star at the table."

Howell returned the grin. "Well, Mr. Cass, if you have need of anythin' while in town, look me up." He then pushed through the batwings to disappear outside.

The crowd around Cody drifted back to the bar and their drinks as he turned and retrieved his money stacked beside the cards still lying on the table. The bills totaled forty-six. A small profit for the evening—even if the method of winning was a bit unexpected.

CHAPTER

‖‖‖‖‖‖‖‖‖‖‖‖‖‖‖‖‖‖‖‖ **2** ‖‖‖‖‖‖‖‖‖‖‖‖‖‖‖‖‖‖‖‖

Take those bags down and pack them carefully into the coach." Jay Gould's voice echoed down the hotel's halls as Cody walked up the stairs to take up his post. It was impossible to overlook the distress and anger in the railroad magnate's voice. "And be quick about it. The sooner I'm away from this stinkhole of ignorance and myopic vision, the better!"

Doubling his pace, Cody reached the head of the stairs and hurried down the hallway. When he rounded the last dogleg, he saw Gould gesturing with his arms while two black bellboys in green-and-gold livery struggled to carry twelve pieces of luggage. Somehow the pair managed to balance the awkward burden, and with mouths twisted in concentration they began to waddle toward Cody.

Hands on his hips, Gould stood glaring at the two. His gaze then lifted, and he stared past the bellboys at Cody. Lifting an arm, he waved the Ranger forward. "You! Come here!"

Cody's own gaze darted to his fellow Ranger, Aaron Hayden, who stood behind the mogul. Hayden silently shook his head and shrugged, indicating he had no idea what Gould wanted. Cody briskly stepped down the narrow hall.

"Yes, sir?" Cody asked when he reached Gould.

Gould didn't reply. Stroking a beard that extended well below his chin, he studied Cody and then Hayden as though he were a man inspecting livestock. Finally he jabbed a finger at Cody. "I've no further need of you. You're dismissed as of this moment.'' Without further explanation he turned and thrust the same finger at Hayden. ''You will proceed with my wife and me. Have your own bags ready as quickly as possible. I have no desire to prolong my stay in this godawful town any longer than is absolutely necessary. Not one moment longer. Do you understand?''

''Understood,'' Hayden answered.

''Good.'' Gould pivoted. ''My wife still has a few items to pack. Meet us downstairs in fifteen minutes.'' He stepped back into the room and slammed the door behind him.

Cody stared at Hayden. ''I think I've just been fired,'' he said dryly.

Hayden scowled with disgust. ''Wish I had your damn luck. I didn't know when I signed on with the Rangers that I'd end up wet-nursing men I'd normally deal with on the end of my fist!'' Hayden shook his head, his expression one of unbridled disdain. ''If I don't throw my things together and get my ass downstairs, that little bastard just might have the driver leave without me.''

''What's going on?'' Cody asked as he walked with Hayden toward their shared chamber.

Hayden opened the door to their room and crossed to the wardrobe. ''Seems Jefferson's city fathers decided they didn't think much of Mr. Gould's proposal,'' he replied as he began stuffing his clothing into a valise. ''They apparently spent most of the night holed up in the city hall, weighing the pros and cons of the offer.''

Cody whistled softly. ''I was out and about last night and never got wind of any meeting.''

Hayden grinned. ''Neither did Gould, or you could've bet your last dime that he'd have been there. Anyway, the outcome of the meeting was that the mayor and the city council paid our little friend a wake-up call about an hour ago to announce that he could take his railroad and put it where the sun don't shine.''

Cody pulled out his own carpetbag and started packing. ''I'll send Major Jones a report on all that's happened. Gould give any indication where he was heading?''

"A town called Marshall." Hayden tugged a pocket watch from his vest and thumbed it open. "If I don't get downstairs, that telegram will say we've *both* been dismissed by Mr. Jay Gould. And I don't think the major'd look kindly on that."

Hayden closed the valise and buckled it. "Will you be heading back to San Antonio?"

"Unless the major's pulled another assignment out of the blue." Now that Gould had abruptly cut him free, Cody needed to tie up loose ends here with a wire to Ranger headquarters in San Antonio, then gather supplies—including a horse—for the long ride back there. After that, he'd have to hope that Diego Alvarez had left enough trail for him to pick up.

Hayden grimaced as he left the room with Cody at his heels. "San Antonio sounds a damned sight better than Marshall— wherever Marshall is."

Cody silently agreed. He had heard of the East Texas town, but that was all.

The two Rangers caught up with Gould and his wife in the lobby. At the registration desk Gould angrily scribbled something into the guest register, then shoved pen and book at the clerk with a grunt. Glancing over a shoulder at Hayden, he snapped, "It's time we were going."

As Gould took his wife's arm and led her to the coach waiting in front of the hotel, Hayden gave Cody's hand a hasty pump. "Good luck, Cody. Maybe we'll work together again sometime."

"Maybe," Cody answered, knowing that the possibility was remote but still a possibility.

He stood in the doorway and watched his colleague climb into the coach with his two wards. Hayden had barely been given time to close the door before Gould called out for the driver to get under way. The team of four horses strained against their harnesses, pulling the coach down the brick-paved street.

"What'd he mean by this?"

Cody glanced around at the desk clerk. "Beg pardon?"

The clerk pointed at the guest book and nodded. "What's that Gould fellow mean by this?"

Cody walked to the desk. The clerk rotated the book and placed a finger beside the words Gould had scrawled: JEFFERSON IS DEAD.

"What's he mean?" the clerk repeated.

Cody pursed his lips and shrugged. "Maybe he thinks he's predicting the future."

"Predicting the future? That don't make no sense. Anyone can see this city ain't dead. Ain't no place bigger in all of Texas."

Cody shrugged again. "I guess he thinks that unless the railroad comes to Jefferson, the future will pass it by."

The clerk snorted. "What a jackass! Who does that bearded old fool think he is, anyway?"

The fact that Gould was one of the more powerful men in the United States obviously didn't impress the clerk. Not that Cody had been impressed by the man, either.

"Don't the man have eyes?" the clerk continued, laughing. "As long as we have the river, we'll do just fine here in Jefferson without Mr. Jay Gould and his damned railroad."

Cody smiled. "That sure seems to be the case." He turned from the desk and walked outside. He had a report to wire to San Antonio.

The clerk probably was right, he told himself as he walked to the telegraph office. The logjam that fed water into the Cypress showed no sign of ever being dislodged from its age-old repose, despite innumerable attempts. As long as that jam rerouted water, Jefferson would keep its riverboat trade—and the railroads had done nothing to hurt cities built on rivers.

Cody pushed back the derby—he'd get rid of this damn foolish outfit as soon as he went back to his room—and glanced overhead. Ominous-looking clouds were gathering to the south. Unless he missed his bet, rain would be falling before the day was out.

He quickened his pace.

•   •   •

Cody handed the second mate of the riverboat, which bore the name *Big Cypress Runner*, four two-bit pieces and stepped across the prow gangplank. It was a whim, a lark, something to occupy the Ranger's time while he waited for storm-downed telegraph lines to be repaired between Jefferson and San Antonio. Without those lines he was temporarily stuck in East Texas to await orders from Major Jones.

Whim it might be, Cody admitted while he followed the mate up the forward stairs and into the main cabin on the boat's second level, but it was also something he had wanted to do since first reading about the luxurious stern-wheelers that traveled the Mississippi River. If he had to blame someone for this bit of folly, the Ranger let it fall on Mark Twain, whose books and other writings Cody devoured whenever they came his way.

"You got about fifteen minutes before we cast off," the second mate said. "That should give you time enough for a quick look-see around."

"Time enough," the Ranger agreed, though he wasn't certain.

"Once we're under way, work yourself down to the lower deck and come up forward," the second mate continued. "As soon as we reach the second bend, you got to be ready to scurry over. It'll be an easy jump to the sandbar."

"I'll be there."

"Make sure you are." The second mate's tone deepened. "A dollar ain't enough to get me in hot water with the captain. And I guarantee he'll toss you over the side—and me with you—if he discovers you've stowed away aboard his ship."

Cody grinned. "Don't worry. I don't have any business in Louisiana. I just want to see what a riverboat feels like."

The second mate nodded. "All right. Just see to it that you're forward when we reach the second bend."

With that the river man turned and hurried down the stairs. Cody watched him, a pleased smile on his face. He felt a rush of excitement, much like the thrill a child feels on Christmas morning. For a dollar bribe he had bought himself a few minutes aboard the riverboat. He'd look around, take a short ride—to get the feel of a boat's deck beneath his feet—then jump off at the sandbar and walk back to Jefferson.

Cody turned and pushed through the double doors that opened into the *Big Cypress Runner*'s main cabin. He looked carefully around the long, narrow room, feeling a brief sensation of regret as he took in the austere amenities the vessel offered. Maybe the dollar he had given the second mate had been thrown away.

Here on a riverboat's second deck opulence was the rule rather than the exception—or at least that was the way of it in everything Cody had read. The magnificent paddle wheelers that populated the Mississippi and Missouri rivers were renowned for the palatial decor of their main saloons. Crystal chandeliers and stained-glass skylights lit these elegant rooms during night or day. Casinos, lounges, and immense dining rooms as well as dance floors to accommodate brass or string bands were customarily found in main cabins for the enjoyment and entertainment of those traveling aboard.

But the Big Cypress Creek wasn't the Mississippi, and this small stern-wheeler wasn't one of the floating palaces that journeyed along the major rivers.

The saloon of the *Big Cypress Runner* was a simple, elongated room with double doors forward and aft that allowed passengers access to the walkway encircling the deck outside. Near those forward doors was a plain, varnished cherrywood bar lacking the ornate craftsmanship Cody expected to see. The remainder of the room was filled with tables, each covered with a white linen tablecloth and surrounded by four neatly placed chairs. A wide aisle running down the center of the main cabin separated the tables to allow waiters to easily move through at mealtimes.

Lining the starboard and port walls of the main saloon were a series of doors with an open transom above each. On the face of every door, painted in gold, was the name of a sovereign state in the Union. This practice of naming the passenger rooms, Cody knew, had given rise to calling the compartments "staterooms."

Cody walked halfway down the center aisle and turned right

at a stateroom bearing the name *Illinois*. Peering in the open door, he studied the room. The interior was as bleak as the main cabin had hinted it would be. A two-level bunk bed pressed against one wall, and two chairs and a small reading table sat across the room. Those were the ten-by-ten-foot room's only furnishings. A narrow door to the left opened on a cramped closet and washbasin.

Suddenly a high-pitched shriek split the air outside and reverberated through the stateroom. Twice more the near-deafening steam whistle blasted, announcing that the *Big Cypress Runner*'s journey downstream was under way.

So much for the "look-see," Cody thought as he moved back into the main saloon. Stepping outside through the double doors at the rear of the long room, he walked to the starboard side, strolling halfway along the walkway before leaning against the rail and gazing at the shore. The deck beneath his feet gently rolled as the stern-wheeler backed away from the dock, then swung northward.

Jefferson and its wharves receded as the riverboat ponderously moved upstream. The last light of day filtered through the feathery leaves of bald cypress trees, whose limbs canopied over half the Big Cypress's width. Leaning over the rail, Cody looked up. Evening stars twinkled in a blue-black sky.

He eased from the whitewashed railing and stepped toward the prow of the stern-wheeler. Here and there he passed an occasional passenger strolling around the deck, but the majority of the boat's travelers seemed to be inside the main cabin, waiting at the tables to be served their evening meal.

Reaching the forward section of the walkway, Cody again paused and leaned against the rail. Below crewmen scurried about with torches held high, lighting running lights that were little more than baskets filled with pine knots. Amid the bales of cotton and wooden crates spread over the first deck, passengers who couldn't afford the questionable luxury of a stateroom shuffled through the cargo in search of a nook or cranny that might provide shelter for the night.

Cody was grateful that he wasn't among those so consigned. As spartan as the *Big Cypress Runner*'s accommodations were, they were far superior to spending the night curled up on a bale of cotton or wedged between two packing crates—though, the Ranger admitted, a cotton bale was far more comfortable than the hard ground of the trail that was often his bed. Still, this particular riverboat was a far cry from the romantic image painted in the pulp pages of the nickel-horribles.

The massive wooden paddle wheel at the stern of the steamer slowed as the riverboat pushed halfway into a sharp right-angled bend in the Big Cypress Creek. The huge wheel churned in reverse, swinging the riverboat about slightly to accommodate the narrow twist in the river. When the wheel once more plowed forward, the *Big Cypress Runner* eased through the bend.

The flickering yellow glow cast by the running lights illuminated the edge of a quarter-mile-long sandbar ahead to Cody's right. Incoming riverboats were required to stop here before docking in Jefferson, he had learned from the second mate, and passengers and crew disembarked and underwent fumigation for lice and fleas. With the discovery that insects could carry contagious disease, most ports demanded that passengers undergo such fumigation before being allowed to leave a riverboat and enter a city.

Cody glanced around. Except for the silhouettes of trees against the star-speckled sky, little remained to be seen. He had delayed the inevitable for as long as he could. It was time to find the second mate and prepare for his leap onto the upcoming sandbar.

With a final glance behind, the Ranger started down the stairs leading to the lower deck, his right hand resting on the stairway's polished wood rail and his left foot reaching for the first step.

Then hell erupted around him.

A roar like the blasts of a hundred cannons shattered the quiet night. Actinic light seared across his eyes, blinding him. An invisible fist of heat slammed into his chest, and a cry of shock and pain was ripped from his lips.

Explosion! Cody's panic-reeling mind grasped a single straw of reason.

A second deafening blast rent the air, and another unseen fist slammed his body from forehead to toes. The force jerked him from the deck and sent him careening through space.

CHAPTER
3

Cody's arms flailed the empty air as he tumbled head over heels, but he found nothing to cling to and halt his precarious flight. Again his brain managed to grasp a straw of reason amid the roiling panic: The force that had hurled him backward was the blast from an explosion. What, why, or how the explosion had occurred eluded him.

Sharp, knifing pain lanced into his side, and abruptly his flight ended. Somewhere through the reverberating roar of the blast still echoing within his head he heard the crack of splintering wood. His body swayed as though he were dangling from a tree limb.

Gritting his teeth, fighting the throbbing pain in his left side, he forced his eyelids open—only to realize that they already *were* open. But he saw nothing except for the blinding flare that had been etched on his retinas. Moaning, he closed his eyes.

He was blind! Temporarily or permanently, he didn't know. Cody's nostrils flared as the acrid smell of smoke filled his nose. He sucked down a deep breath to quell the terror that tightened his chest. Mindless panic wouldn't serve a blind man aboard a burning riverboat.

His eyes flew open again, but the searing, white image of the explosion still robbed him of sight. He cursed loudly, frustration and anger edging back panic. This was no place for a blind man—wherever *this* was. He had to get help and fast.

He called out. Silence answered. Again, he called, and again . . .

His fear had numbed his still-functioning senses. Chaos reigned all around him, the cries and screams of men and women piercing the darkness, each a desperate plea for aid. Who would hear his own call for help?

"Over the side! Everybody get over the side and swim for the banks!" a deep voice shouted. "Abandon ship! Everybody abandon ship!"

Cody shifted toward the voice, and when he did, his body swayed and bobbed, and once more he heard the dry cracking of splintering wood. Freezing, he remained motionless until the swaying stopped. Whatever had snagged him from his head-over-heels flight felt dangerously close to breaking.

He tried calling out again. Still no one answered him. *Think!* he ordered himself. The riverboat was burning, sinking. Orders had been given to abandon ship. He had to get himself into the water without help from the passengers and crew, who, from the sound of splashing water below, were occupied with saving their own lives.

"Tom, forget the black gang," a voice said from below Cody. "Ain't nobody left in there. The boiler went. Save your own hide. We ain't paid enough to give a damn 'bout nobody on this bucket 'cept ourselves. Now, git your ass over the side."

The voice had supplied the reason for the explosion: an exploded boiler—that most feared calamity of riverboat travel. The knowledge did nothing to relieve Cody's own predicament.

"Help!" he called out. "I'm up here and need help!"

The sound of two heavy splashes—bodies striking the river—answered him. Apparently the unseen Tom had taken the advice and jumped overboard with the man who had told him to save his own hide. Not that Cody blamed them. It was his own hide that occupied his own thoughts at the moment.

He opened his eyes again and turned his head from side to side. Nothing. He swallowed hard, forcing back the panic that welled within him anew. It was as though a layer of gauze was wrapped over his eyes. But beyond the gauze he thought he could discern shapes now. He blinked—once, twice, three times. The gauzy veil faded to a milky film. Blurred though it was, he could see again.

What he saw was far from comforting.

The tree limb that had broken his careening flight through the air was, in fact, the walkway's rail, and the force of his body hitting it had torn it from the support columns. It jutted into the air, precariously extending over the main deck at a forty-five-degree angle.

Cody cautiously turned his neck and glanced toward his feet. His heart doubled its beat, pounding like a bass drum.

That the rail remained attached to the deck was nothing short of a miracle and testimony to the workmanship that had gone into the *Big Cypress Runner*'s construction. Half-exposed nails, twisted and bent beneath his weight, were all that held the rail and himself in place. The dry cracking he had heard when he moved was the sound of tortured wood ripping away from those nails. The rail was ready to give way beneath him and send his body plummeting headfirst to the main deck fifteen feet below.

Taking a couple of deep breaths to steady himself, Cody edged backward toward the dubious security of the sinking riverboat's deck. His movement set the rail swaying and groaning as it tried to separate itself from twisted iron. Doing his best to overlook the inevitable outcome should the rail give way before he reached the deck, Cody eased downward a fraction of an inch at a time.

Wood cracked and splintered to his left. The rail jerked and sagged beneath him. Reacting rather than thinking, Cody rolled to the upper deck. His body flopped belly down on solid wood as the rail shuddered, then collapsed, crashing to the main deck below.

Closing his eyes, the Ranger let out a breath in a soft whistle. That had been closer than he liked to think about. But he wasn't out of danger yet. He still remained aboard a burning riverboat on a one-way course for the muddy bottom of the

Big Cypress. If he wanted to see the dawning of another day, he had to get himself off the boat—and the sooner, the better.

Ignoring the pain of his bruised ribs, Cody stood up. A milky film clouded his eyes, but this cloud was smoke, not a residue left from staring into the face of the exploding boiler. He looked quickly around. To his left yellow and orange flames licked up from the lower deck. He pivoted to the right, ready to leap over the side and join the passengers and crew already swimming for the safety of the riverbanks.

"Help!" a woman's voice cried from behind him. "Somebody help me! Please! Help!"

He twisted around, blinking against the smoke burning his eyes. He cocked his head right and left, straining to locate the source of the cry.

"Please, anyone!" the woman called out again. "I can't move! Please, help me!"

Cody's gaze darted to the right and alighted on the door to the main cabin, which lay half torn from its hinges. The harsh glow of raging fire came from within the saloon—and so did the voice. The Ranger hesitated only an instant before darting through the entrance.

"Where are you?" he shouted. The glare of the flames devouring the center of the room and the heavy smoke all but blinded him. "I can't see you!"

"Here!" The woman's voice came from his right. "I'm here! Please, help me!"

Squinting, Cody peered through the swirling haze of smoke. An arm thrust out from beneath a jumble of tables and chairs that had been thrown against the stateroom doors by the blast.

"Here!" Hope edged aside the desperation in the woman's voice. "Here! I'm over here! I'm pinned down and can't move!"

Stepping over the bloody, twisted body of a man in a dark business suit, Cody crossed to the small mountain of tables and chairs and began tossing them aside. More than furniture trapped the woman; he dragged away the bodies of a young man and an old woman before he reached the owner of the voice that had called to him.

"Are you hurt?" he asked, kneeling beside a woman who appeared to be in her midtwenties. "Can you walk?"

"I think so." She nodded with uncertainty and sat up. "I don't think either one of us is injured."

It was only then that Cody noticed the blanket-wrapped bundle clutched in the woman's right arm. She moved aside a corner of that blanket to reveal the face of an infant.

"We both seem to be all right"—the woman looked up and smiled at her rescuer—"thanks to you."

"If you're going to remain that way, we have to get out of here." Taking the baby from her and holding it securely in his left arm, Cody helped the young woman to her feet. "Can you swim?"

"Since I was five. My daddy taught me down in—"

Cutting short her life's history, Cody grabbed her arm and pulled her toward the main cabin's forward door. "You'll have to jump into the river from this deck and then swim for the bank. Fire's all over the lower level."

"But Elizabeth . . ." the woman protested as they stepped onto the walkway. "She's just three months old! How is she—"

"I'll take care of Elizabeth," Cody said, again cutting her off. The sooner all three of them were off the *Big Cypress Runner,* the better he'd feel about their chances of surviving this night.

Moving away from the flames that now danced over the riverboat's port side, he maneuvered the young woman to the right. When they reached the railing, he helped her climb onto it. "Leap out as far as you can, then swim for the bank."

She glanced down at Cody, staring at the infant cradled in his arm. Her forehead creased with worry.

"Your daughter will be all right; I promise you that. Now, jump!" Cody urged.

She turned and gazed at the dark water below, but hesitated, uncertain of the height or the fate of her child left in the arms of a total stranger.

"Jump!"

To encourage action, he placed a hand on her backside and

shoved. A cry of alarm trailed the woman as she fell, then abruptly ended when she struck the river.

For moments that seemed to stretch to hours Cody leaned over the rail and peered below. When the young woman's head bobbed to the surface, he called out, "Swim for the bank! I'm right behind you."

He then climbed onto the rail, balancing there while he shifted the child in his left arm to his chest and clutched it with both arms.

Metal groaned and wood creaked. The riverboat listed to the starboard.

Cody's intention to leap from the rail feet first changed without warning. The boat's death throes catapulted him forward, plummeting him head downward toward the water. In midair he drew himself into a ball to curl protectively around the infant he carried. He struck the inky river with his shoulders, like a misfired cannonball.

Repressing the natural urge to use arms and legs to struggle for the surface as he sank toward the river's bottom, he held his breath and waited for his body's buoyancy to carry him upward. Only then did he uncurl and kick toward the surface. As his head broke the surface, he thrust both arms upward, holding the child high above the water. Dark eyes surrounded by a baby-fat, pink face blinked down at him, looking completely unaffected by—or too startled to react to—the unexpected plunge into the river.

"Hang on, little one," Cody said softly. "I'll have you back with your momma in a few minutes."

He rolled onto his back and sat the child on his chest, then used his legs to propel them toward the bank. The young woman stood waist deep in the water waiting for them. She snatched her baby from Cody's chest and hugged the infant close to her own breast while tears streamed down her cheeks. Cody stood and helped mother and child onto dry land, then seated them beneath a cypress tree. He then turned back to the river.

"Help!" a man shouted from midstream. "My leg's hurt! I can't make it!"

Because of the reflected flames dancing on the river's surface, it took Cody a minute to locate the man. Then he spotted his head bobbing halfway to the sinking riverboat, and an arm rose out of the water and jerked from side to side.

"I can't keep afloat!" the man cried out.

Cody reached the river in three quick strides and bounded into the water. Legs kicking furiously and arms stretching out in long, powerful strokes, the Ranger reached the man's side in less than a minute.

"Roll to your back," he ordered, prepared for a quick blow to the wounded man's chin should he suddenly panic. "Relax. I'll get you to safety."

But the man readily complied, shifting to his back. Cody slipped an arm around the man's chest and began swimming toward the bank. A couple of yards from land two men, crewmen by their dress, splashed into the water and took the wounded man from him.

Cody stood once more and stared back at the burning boat. Two women, weighted down by their dresses, struggled to reach the bank. Once more the Ranger dived back into the river, helping one and then the other into the shallows.

Barely stopping to catch his breath between each rescue mission, Cody assisted five other passengers and crew members to safety. Suddenly a high-pitched cry of alarm pulled his attention back to the flaming steamer. His eyes scanned first the riverboat and then the water for the source of the cry. He saw no one.

"Here!" a woman called, her voice thin with terror. "I'm here! I can't swim! Help me!"

Cody still couldn't spot the woman.

"Here! Please, anyone! I can't swim!"

Flames leapt high from the *Big Cypress Runner*'s Texas deck, and light cascaded over the water.

There! Cody saw her now. Amid the spilled cargo that floated near the listed craft, an elderly woman clung to a bobbing crate.

"I see you!" he shouted. "Hold on! I'll be there!"

Again he threw himself into the water, arms stretching out

and legs kicking. He swam to the middle of the river, weaving through the debris that now cluttered his path.

"Here!" the woman called out. "I'm over here."

Cody lifted his head and treaded water until he located the stranded woman and the crate she clutched. He covered the twenty feet separating them in a matter of seconds.

"Float on your back, and I'll take you to shore," he instructed as he grabbed the crate and let its buoyancy support him. "Just remain calm. I'll keep your head above the water. There's nothing to be afraid of. Now, release the crate and roll to your back."

"No." The woman's head shook with determination.

Cody doubled his fist. He had no desire to strike a woman—especially one old enough to be his grandmother—but if a well-placed jab to the chin was what it took to save her life, then he was prepared to deliver it.

"Take the boy first," the woman said before Cody could unleash a punch. "He can't swim either. I can hold on longer. He's growing tired."

"Boy?" Cody's eyes widened, then narrowed. How many children had been aboard the *Big Cypress Runner*? "Where is he?"

"On the opposite side." The woman inclined her head to the right. "I don't know who he belongs to. I grabbed hold of him just before he went under."

Cody maneuvered around the crate and found a boy no older than three clinging to the wood, water lapping around him. The child's eyes were huge with fear.

"Little one"—Cody kept his voice soft and steady—"everything's going to be all right now. I'm going to carry you to shore. It'll be just like taking a piggyback ride. You like riding piggyback, don't you?"

Looking uncertain, the boy nodded solemnly.

"Good. Now all you have to do is climb onto my back and wrap your arms around my neck." Cody would never have given an adult such a stranglehold on him, but a three-year-old boy was a different matter. "You can do that, can't you?"

Again the child nodded, and he slipped onto the offered back when Cody shifted in the water.

Patting the boy's hands as they tightened around his neck, Cody said, "Now, just hang on tight, and I'll have you out of this water in a couple of minutes."

He glanced at the woman. "And you hang on tight, too. I'll be back as fast as I can."

The woman smiled weakly, though it was evident she was terrified. "I'll be here. I'm not going anywhere."

Returning the smile, Cody nodded and released the crate. In wide-sweeping breaststrokes, he swam through the bobbing debris. The child on his back kept his arms firmly locked about Cody's neck, but he neither cried nor whimpered. He was either real brave or too frightened to make a sound, Cody decided.

Another explosion blasted the night. Light once again flared over the river. Half turning to look over his shoulder, Cody watched as a column of flame leapt from the riverboat's burning upper deck. The boat listed, then listed again. White-capped waves rippled out as half the vessel sank beneath the water. Cargo crates that had bobbed in the river now jerked violently as the waves threw them from side to side.

"No!" the woman behind him screamed.

Cody watched in horror as a large crate shot forward, slamming into the small box the woman clung to. There was no escape; she was caught between the two. She screamed again. The scream then faded to a muffled moan.

As rapidly as the two crates struck, they careened off each other. The woman no longer clutched the smaller one. Her arms weakly flailed the water some five feet from the box that had supported her.

Scissoring his legs, Cody swung himself about. As fast as he could move, he swam toward the woman. It wasn't fast enough. Her head slipped beneath the surface. The old wives' tale about a drowning person going down three times was nothing more than that. Not even bubbles remained when Cody reached the spot where he had seen her sink. Had he not had the child on his back, he would have tried to retrieve her from the inky depths. But there was a three-year-old boy clutching his neck—the child she had demanded be saved before herself.

Once again he twisted around in the water and swam for the bank. He told himself there was only so much a lone man could do. It didn't help. Rootless guilt knotted his gut, and he damned himself with blame. If only he had been quicker. Why hadn't he tried to drag the crate to shore with the woman and child clinging to it?

A hundred alternatives plagued his brain as he stepped from the water with the boy still riding his back. Reaching the cypress trunk where the mother and child he had first brought from the riverboat still sat, he placed the boy beside the young woman.

"Will you look after this little one? I don't know where his parents are."

The woman looked up, smiled, then cuddled the boy to her. "I'll take care of him," she said gently.

"Thank you." Cody stood and turned back to the river.

For a moment tongues of fire leapt toward the starry sky; then the *Big Cypress Runner* listed one last time before sinking beneath the water. The darkness of night closed over the river, bringing with it an unexpected chill.

Whether the gooseflesh that rippled up and down his arms came from the night's coolness or from having stared death in the face, Cody wasn't certain. He told himself that it didn't matter. All that mattered was that he was alive and would see the sun rise on a new day. But he lied to himself. He couldn't escape the image of the woman sinking beneath the water, never to rise.

CHAPTER

4

Coffee?"

Cody opened his eyes, shoving back the vision of a drowning woman that had haunted him through the long hours of the night. The tortured image vanished, but not the hollow sense that had emptied him. A brave woman had died, and he found no rhyme or reason in that death—only waste. Death was never more a waste than when it came without reason.

"Coffee?" a female voice asked again. "You look like you could use a cup."

Cody glanced up to see two young women—no, not women; both were no more than bright-eyed, pink-faced girls in their teens—carrying a steaming bucket between them. One ladled a white-enameled tin cup into the bucket and held it out for him to take.

"It's freshly made. Just brought it from town," a girl with long blond pigtails said. "My momma made it. Folks say she's one of the best cooks in this part of Texas."

"Thank you." He accepted the cup and took a tentative sip. When he noticed the look of anticipation on the girl's face, he added, "It's very good. Tell your momma thank you for me."

She brightened, then looked at her companion and nodded. The two hurried along the bank to offer hot coffee to the next stranded passenger they came upon.

Taking another sip, Cody watched them for several moments. How fresh and clean they appeared in their crisply ironed, bright summer dresses. And how incongruous they were with the muddy scene surrounding them. Cody looked around. Not even the morning light had improved the situation.

Mist smelling of smoke floated through the bald cypresses and hung over the river's surface. The *Big Cypress Runner*'s twin smokestacks thrusting up from the water were the only visible remains of the riverboat. Along both banks wooden crates had been washed ashore like flotsam after a flood, and here and there men waded into the water to retrieve crates that hadn't found their way to shore.

Cody's gaze moved up and down both banks. Passengers and crew members alike sat and stared at the river, dazed disbelief on their faces. They were alive, somehow having escaped death that had claimed others last night, but why or how they had been spared was unclear.

Townsfolk who had come running when they had heard the explosions that had ripped apart the riverboat's boiler now moved among the survivors with coffee and sandwiches. Wagons had been promised at sunrise to take the survivors back to town, but they had yet to arrive.

"Here. Use that coffee to wash these down." Sheriff Manly Howell squatted beside Cody and opened a napkin in his hand to reveal two fried-egg sandwiches. "You need to keep up your strength."

Cody accepted one and took a bite. It was warm and peppery. He nodded his thanks, saying, "What I need is a hot bath, a shave, and about twenty-four hours of sleep."

Howell tore the remaining sandwich in two and took a bite from one of the halves. "I'd like you to hold off on that sleep awhile, if you don't mind."

The strength to hike a questioning eyebrow was all the energy Cody could muster.

"I know you helped out a lot here last night and must be bone weary"—the sheriff paused to swallow—"but I had a chat with Shorty Parsons, our town telegrapher last night. He said a railroad agent was in yesterday to send a message to a Texas Ranger commandant by the name of Major Jones.

Shorty said that man signed his name as Cody rather than Cass, like he'd been callin' himself. That true?''

Cody took the last bite from the sandwich, nodding as he chewed. Reaching into his pocket, he pulled out a large gold pocket watch, the kind known as a turnip. He thumbed it open, surprised to find the timepiece still running after the swim in the river. In the watch's cover, protected from the water by its glass frame, was a sepia photograph of a lovely young woman.

"Your gal?" the sheriff asked.

"A sweet memory," Cody replied. He lied. He had no idea who she was. The photograph had been in the watch when he first bought it, and he had continued to use it to hide the hollowed-out compartment behind. Now, lifting out the metal-rimmed photograph, Cody revealed a five-pointed star set in a silver circle. The Ranger badge had been hand carved from a Mexican ten-peso piece.

Howell whistled softly as he studied the badge and then eyed Cody for a moment, as though sizing him up for the first time. "I reckoned you for a Ranger after what Shorty said. Guess you're here 'cause of them threats Gould received?"

Cody confirmed the sheriff's evaluation. "Name's Cody, not Cass. No reason to keep that from you now."

The lawman glanced around and heaved a sigh. "Well, Mr. Cody, I've got a fine mess on my hands here and could use the help of a Texas Ranger."

"Don't you have deputies for that?" Cody asked, then took a sip of coffee.

"Four of 'em, to be exact—but with somethin' like this, they ain't enough. Two of my men are on twenty-four-hour duty in town until further notice. The other two'll be pullin' the same hours until the wreckage can be raised and the river cleared for boats waitin' to move in and out of the city. That should take 'bout three days or so—if everythin' goes off without a hitch. . . ."

Cody groaned inwardly. He hadn't considered the possibility of working again so quickly. Not after all he had gone through last night.

"I think you can see my predicament. I need a trained man to give me a hand clearin' all this up—locatin' the survivors and identifyin' the dead." Howell's eyebrows arched expectantly.

"I suppose this is to be volunteer work," Cody said, scanning the river scene. What the sheriff asked wouldn't be physically hard, just time-consuming.

"Best I can offer is a bed and three meals a day and a promise you'll have a berth on the first boat headin' downstream as soon as the river's clear. My budget can't handle any more than that." Howell's eyebrows remained arched with hope.

"I'd like a couple hours in that bed before I get started," Cody replied. "It's been a long night." Until he heard from Major Jones, he was stuck in Jefferson anyway, he supposed. And Rangers always helped out the local law when needed.

"Be easier if we started now," Howell answered, nodding toward a nearby group of passengers gathered around the two girls and their bucket of coffee. "Soon as these folks begin headin' back into town, it'll be hard to track 'em all down."

Like it or not, Cody realized that the lawman was right. If the business at hand was to identify the survivors and casualties of the wreck, now was the time to do it.

He sighed wearily. "All right. We start now."

Howell smiled as he reached into a shirt pocket and pulled out a folded piece of yellow paper, handing it to Cody along with a sharpened pencil. "Had the booking agent make me two copies of the passenger list. You can work this bank. I'll take the other side."

Cody unfolded the sheet of paper and scanned the double column of handwritten names. "What about the crew and staff?"

"We'll have to meet with some of the *Big Cypress Runner*'s officers and work that up later," Howell replied with a shrug. "The passenger list's a beginnin', at least. Print an *S* beside them that's livin' for 'survivor' and a *D* beside them that didn't make it." The sheriff peered at Cody. "I didn't notice either a Cass or a Cody on that list. How come you were on board?''

Cody explained his ill-timed lark the night before. Taking a final swig of coffee, he stood and said, ''Guess we might as well get started.''

It had been a long, exhausting day. It was nearing six o'clock when, on legs that felt more like lead than flesh and bone, Cody walked out of the hot, stuffy telegraph office into the hot, humid East Texas evening. The visit to the telegrapher had been a waste of time. The lines were still down between Jefferson and San Antonio, which meant that any messages to or from Major Jones still hadn't gotten through, and the telegrapher couldn't say when they would.

Cody trudged down the street toward the sheriff's office, his arms hanging like deadweights at his side. He was still in need of a shave and a bath, but right now he'd settle for Howell's promised supper and a bed to stretch out on. Sleep was what he needed more than anything—to forget the terror he had seen in the eyes of the survivors and to erase the blank stares of the dead.

''Thirty dead you say is the official count, Manly?'' A man in a rumpled white suit with mud-caked boots was standing before the sheriff's desk when Cody entered the office. The man glanced at the newcomer, nodded, then looked back at Howell.

''Best as we can make it right now, Ed,'' Howell replied. His gaze moved to Cody. ''This here's Sam Cody. He was on the *Big Cypress Runner* last night. Been helpin' me out today. Cody, meet Ed Dupree, editor of our local newspaper.''

Dupree stuck out a hand, and Cody shook it. ''Mind if I interview you after I'm through with Manly, Mr. Cody? I'd like to do a piece on what it was like to be aboard the riverboat last night.''

Cody collapsed into a chair on the right side of the office, his body sagging with weariness. ''I'm afraid I'll have to pass,

Mr. Dupree. The sheriff promised he'd buy me supper, and then I intend to climb into bed and sleep for a year or five.''

A disappointed shadow flickered over Dupree's face, but then he shrugged and turned back to the lawman. ''Any names among the dead I'd recognize, Manly?''

Howell lifted a piece of paper from his desk and glanced over it. Eventually he shook his head. ''Just everyday people here. Mostly members of the black gang who were working the boiler when it blew.''

''Then the *Big Cypress Runner* did go down because the boiler exploded?'' the newspaperman asked.

''Ripped a hole big enough to drive a wagon through in the main deck and hull,'' the lawman answered. ''Did about the same thing to the main cabin and the Texas deck. Luckily most of the passengers escaped the blast.''

Cody closed his eyes. One woman passenger had escaped that blast—only to be drowned between floating debris. He had stared long and hard at the four dead women who had been pulled from the river, but he recognized none of them. A hollowness emptied him; he'd never know the name of the old woman who had given her life so that a three-year-old boy might live. Her courage deserved a greater reward than being celebrated only in his memory.

''That should do it for now.'' Dupree slipped his notebook into a pocket and turned to the door. ''I'll double-check everything tomorrow before I set my type.'' As the newspaperman opened the door, he paused and looked back at the sheriff. ''Oh, by the way. Jefferson wasn't the only place in Texas to have all hell break out last night.''

Howell stared at Dupree. ''What d'ya mean?''

''There was a train wreck yesterday evening near a little town called Terrell about seventy or eighty miles this side of Fort Worth.''

Cody lifted his head. ''A Texas and Pacific train?'' He realized how stupid his question was the instant he uttered it. No other railroad line presently operated in Texas.

Dupree apparently didn't notice. He nodded and said, ''An engine pulling five cars—two of them passenger coaches—

jumped the track, according to the wire I received this afternoon. At least twenty people were killed—maybe more.''

"Headin' to or from Fort Worth?'' Howell asked, his tone
more one of politeness than interest.

"Eastbound,'' Dupree replied.

"Don't sound none too good,'' the sheriff said as he leaned
back in his chair. "At least it was on dry land. Damned sight
easier to work than the river.''

Dupree stood at the open door for several silent moments
as though expecting further questions. When none came, he
bid the two good night and stepped outside.

Cody glanced at the sheriff and found him studying the
casualty lists they had compiled. "You mentioned something
about feeding me when I got back from the telegraph office,''
he reminded Howell.

"Hummm,'' Howell mumbled as he continued to scan the
lists.

"You find something interesting?'' Cody asked.

Howell passed the lists to the Ranger. "Not certain. But it
seems neither one of us could account for one of the *Big Cypress Runner*'s passengers.''

Cody found the same unmarked name on both lists. "Mrs.
Calvin Brady. Is that important?''

"Could be, which is why I didn't mention it to Ed,'' the
sheriff answered. "Mrs. Calvin Brady just happens to be Mary
Brady, wife of State Senator Calvin Brady.''

Cody's eyes widened. Calvin Brady had made a name for
himself in Texas right after the Civil War. He was a nail-tough
hombre who had fought off Comanches and Kiowas and built
a ranch that covered nearly half the plains between Fort Worth
and Wichita Falls. Some would call it a cattle empire, Cody
mused.

But livestock wasn't Brady's only interest. The rancher had
been one of the first men to challenge the stranglehold that
northern carpetbaggers had had on Texas following the war.
He had run for the state legislature and won hands down. So
strong was his pro-Texas stand that two years later he was

elected state senator, a seat the forty-five-year-old cattle baron had retained without opposition for three terms.

"Rumor is that Brady's a shoo-in for the governor's mansion come the next election, if he wants it," Howell said. "And there ain't nobody in Texas that believes he don't want it. The only thing he ain't done to make certain the citizens know he's a candidate is come out and announce his intentions."

Cody understood why the sheriff had withheld Mrs. Brady's name from the newspaper editor. "Are you certain Mary Brady was on the *Big Cypress Runner*?"

"Couldn't find anyone who said she was or anyone to say she wasn't. Till I find out one way or the other, I ain't goin' to be the one startin' any rumors—not with Calvin Brady involved. I kinda like my job here"—he winked at Cody—"if you get my drift."

"I get your drift," Cody replied, glad that the missing Mrs. Brady was the lawman's problem and not his own.

"You mentioned something about me promising you supper, didn't you?"

Cody nodded.

"They fry up a pretty decent beefsteak down at the saloon. Think you could handle one?"

"Maybe two," Cody said with a grin. "I haven't had a bite to eat since that egg sandwich this morning."

Howell pushed from his desk and waved Cody toward the door. "Then what are you sittin' there for? You don't get fed in here unless you're restin' in one of my cells."

CHAPTER
5

Cody waited while the livery stable owner hayed the horses. After three days of waiting for the telegraph lines to be repaired, the Ranger had decided it was time to head for San Antonio on his own rather than waste further time. Having accompanied Jay Gould and his wife to Jefferson in their carriage—the assumption being he'd be returning the same way—Cody now found himself needing transportation back to Frontier Battalion headquarters. He'd now be adding the cost of a horse to the taxpayers' tab along with the suit.

The stable owner—Able Venus was his name, according to the sign out front—finished his chore and approached his customer. "How can I help ya?"

Cody smiled. "I reckon I'm open to a little horse trading."

Able sized him up. "You're that feller who come to town with that Jay Gould, ain't ya?"

"That's right."

"How come you didn't leave with him in that fancy carriage of his?"

"It's a long story."

The stable owner rubbed a hand over mouth and chin as though pondering the situation—but the action didn't fool Cody. The hand might've hidden Able's greedy grin of delight, but it didn't conceal the bright dollar signs that sparked in the man's eyes. The Ranger was over a barrel, and Able Venus damned well knew it.

"Just might be able to fix you up," Able finally said. He

stepped toward the rear of the stable, waving the Ranger after him. "I got two geldin's that are damn fine saddle horses, if you want to take a look at 'em."

"I want," Cody answered. He followed the stable owner to adjoining stalls; in one was a sorrel gelding and in the other a buckskin. "Lead 'em out and let me see what you have."

Able brought the chestnut from its stall first. Hand on halter, he led the animal up and down the barn several times while Cody studied the animal's conformation. The sorrel was sleek and lean—built for speed.

"This here's a blooded horse," Able said as he returned the chestnut to its stall. "Kentucky bred and raised. Five years old. A feller brought him down this way hopin' to clean up on a few races. Got hisself shot in a poker game 'fore he ever raced his horse."

Speed was nice in a horse, but on the trail endurance was often more important. A thoroughbred wasn't cut out for traveling the harsh country near the Texas-Mexico border. Cody gestured toward the buckskin. "Let's see your other wares."

The gelding Able brought from the other stall stood fifteen hands and had a head that looked like it belonged on the neck of a draft horse rather than a saddle pony. But the animal's long legs appeared solid. Cody ran a hand down each of the buckskin's legs to confirm what his eyes told him.

"What's his history?" he asked.

"Got him as a colt and broke him myself," Able replied. "Thought about keepin' him for a stud awhile, but I had to cut him when he was two. He was gettin' a little too headstrong. He's four this August."

The stable owner had brought out his goods, and Cody had done his perusing. It was time to get down to brass tacks. The Ranger asked, "What's your price for the buckskin?"

"Two hundred," Able said without a blink.

How the man could keep a straight face while voicing such an outrageous sum amazed Cody. In the time-honored manner of all horse traders Able had opened with his best shot, hardly expecting the Ranger to bite at the price. And Cody didn't expect him to accept his counteroffer, which, also according to tradition, was ridiculously low.

For the next twenty minutes they traded offers and counteroffers. Finally Able reached what apparently was his rock-bottom price. It was fifteen dollars too steep, to Cody's way of thinking, but he'd have to accept it, he supposed.

He was about to agree to the figure when a voice called, "Cody!"

Cody turned to see Manly Howell enter the stable, waving a yellow piece of paper.

"Cody," the lawman called out again, "this just arrived at the telegraph office for you. I thought you might want to take a look at it." The sheriff gulped down several swallows of air to catch his breath as he handed the envelope to the Ranger.

So the telegraph lines had finally been repaired, Cody thought. His brow furrowing, he turned the sealed envelope over and used a fingertip to slit it open. There was only one person the wire could be from.

The message was short. Cody's frown deepened as he read the words once and then a second time. Major Jones had assigned him to a new case—the Texas and Pacific train wreck in Terrell—and he had informed Captain Wallace Vickery in Del Rio that Cody wouldn't be immediately returning to his post. The telegram ended with a wish for a hasty conclusion to the investigation.

It was the heart of the wire that held the Ranger's attention. The Texas and Pacific wreck, which Cody had first learned of the night the *Big Cypress Runner* sank, had been no accident; it had been caused by the removal of a section of track. No robbery had occurred, and no motive for the wanton destruction was readily apparent. Cody's assignment was to apprehend those responsible for the wreck.

"You seem perturbed, Cody. You ain't like that king over there in Greece who kills the messenger who brings bad news, are you?"

Cody glanced up to find Howell staring at him. He smiled at the sheriff. "A change of plans. Seems like I'll be heading west to Terrell rather than south to San Antonio."

"Terrell?" A perplexed expression momentarily crossed Howell's face; then his eyes widened slightly. "The train wreck! I'd forgotten about it."

With a nod Cody added, "Apparently the line's requested Ranger assistance in investigating the wreck."

"Lucky for you I dropped by the telegraph office this mornin', I reckon. . . ."

Cody wasn't certain of his luck. Iron horses weren't the kind of horse he usually dealt with. And north-central Texas wasn't exactly his territory.

"Wouldn't have even gone by, 'cept I was hopin' to get an answer to my telegram," Howell continued.

"Telegram?" Cody questioned halfheartedly. His mind was on the wreck.

Howell's gaze scanned the street outside the barn as though in anticipation of trouble. "Yeah. I wired Senator Brady yesterday, inquirin' about his wife. I explained that her name had been listed among the passengers aboard the *Big Cypress Runner*, but she remained unaccounted for after the sinkin'."

"Anyone verify that she boarded the riverboat?" Cody asked.

Howell shook his head. "Nobody remembers whether she boarded the boat or not. One maid recalls layin' out her stateroom but says she never saw the woman."

"And Brady's answer?"

"No answer yet," the sheriff replied. "Probably too early for one. Some of these small-town telegraphers take their own sweet time about gettin' a wire to someone. I'll give the senator a few more days before tryin' again."

Cody turned to Able Venus, who had been standing there, listening to the conversation. "Guess you've got yourself a deal on the gelding," the Ranger said, reaching into his pocket. He counted out the money and handed it over to Able, who grinned as he stuffed the money in his own pocket.

"Reckon saddlin' up the buckskin for you is included in the price," the stable owner said and hurried to get the horse.

When Able brought out the saddled and bridled buckskin from its stall, Howell extended a hand toward the Ranger.

"Cody, you take care of yourself, you hear? If you ever make it back through Jefferson, take the time and look me up."

Cody shook the lawman's hand. "I'll do that, Sheriff. And you keep your eyes open for tinhorns. A lawman doesn't get paid enough to go and lose it all to a card shark."

Howell chuckled. "I'll do that. Yessir, I'll do that."

Mounting up, Cody reined the buckskin about, then lightly tapped the horse's sides with his silver-spurred heels and headed westward. Two miles out of town he stopped beneath the shade of a towering white oak to unpin the badge from his vest and stash it inside the watch compartment. He then reversed the double-sided leather vest to hide the pinholes. Major Jones's telegram had ordered him to continue the charade of being a railroad investigator—at least until he was certain of the situation in Terrell. The few brief days of openly admitting to being a Ranger were over.

CHAPTER
6

Cody led the gelding back from the small creek the animal had been drinking from, slipped the reins over the horse's head, and mounted up. He looked around. The phrase "rolling plains" had been coined for the land that stretched from horizon to horizon around him. Except for the line of dense bushes and an occasional black willow that hedged the stream to suck precious moisture from its narrow bed, rich and green grassland covered the earth.

Tapping the buckskin's sides with his spurs, Cody swung the horse westward once again, keeping the railroad tracks that cut across the north-central Texas prairie on his left. He had located the tracks shortly after dawn that morning, and since then he never strayed more than a mile north of the line, knowing that no cartographer could have penned a better map to his destination. Sooner or later the rails would bring him to Terrell.

The sooner the better, he thought, shifting his weight in the saddle. He had spent too much time in Jefferson; his body now paid the price for his long hiatus from horseback. His backside felt a twinge of tenderness with every step the buckskin took, and his thighs were stiff and sore from almost three days of twelve-hour stretches in the saddle.

The minor pains plaguing him brought a sense of embarrassment and punctuated the fact that his eight days in Jefferson had been soft duty—far softer than he had realized. Cody liked to believe he kept himself sharpened like the blade of the bowie knife sheathed at his waist. He now felt that edge had been dulled and hoped this new assignment would hone him into condition before he returned to Company C.

Cody's gaze shifted from the green prairie to the railroad tracks. Despite tight muscles and twinges of pain, he much preferred riding horseback to riding steel rails. There was no escaping the fact that the railroads were the country's future— a future that grew closer with each new tie laid—but though Americans could now speed between the Atlantic and Pacific coasts in a matter of days rather than months, they were missing out on the expansive grandeur of the country, which was now seen only as a blurred streak of colors through the window of a passenger car.

The harsh shriek of a steam whistle shattered Cody's reverie. He eased the gelding to a halt as it topped a hill. Another wailing blast from a steam whistle pulled Cody's head around. A locomotive, black smoke billowing from its smokestack, barreled across the prairie, heading eastward with a single passenger car and five boxcars in tow.

Cody frowned, surprised to see the rails in use. Perhaps the wreck hadn't been as serious as he had been led to believe for the tracks to be cleared so soon.

When the train had rumbled past, he scanned the land ahead of him and saw a cluster of wooden buildings sitting on the horizon. Terrell, he thought, estimating that five miles lay between him and the small town. He nudged the buckskin's sides. Another hour's ride separated him from his destination. He wasn't getting any closer sitting atop a hill, staring at the town.

Cluster didn't correctly describe the twenty buildings loosely arrayed on each side of a single, wagon-rutted dirt street that ran east-west for a half mile through Terrell. Whitewashed houses randomly built around the core of the town formed its perimeter, and beyond the houses were the farms and then prairie again. The massive trees—pecans, oaks, and elms—growing beside most of the buildings took Cody by surprise. The town obviously had a plentiful water supply nearby for it to support trees in the middle of a prairie.

Slowly riding the gelding down the street, Cody studied the town. Now and then he drew an idle glance from men and women as they went about their daily routines, but for the most part his arrival went unnoticed. Though he saw no hotel, he did pass a two-story house that sported a shingle proclaiming it to be a boardinghouse. Toward the end of the long street he also saw a large red barn with LIVERY STABLE painted in white on its side. He was relieved. At least there'd be bed and board for both him and the gelding during their stay here.

A quarter of the way down the street he came upon a small, square building constructed from mismatched pieces of limestone. Even without the black and white sign hanging above the door that read SHERIFF, the flat, steel bars across the windows marked the structure as a jail.

For a moment Cody considered turning his mount around back to the boardinghouse, renting a room, and having a good meal and a long sleep before beginning the investigation that had brought him here. It was only a fleeting thought. The day was less than half over, and there was no reason to delay the job at hand.

He reined the buckskin to a line of three hitching posts outside the sheriff's office, dismounted, and tied the reins to a wrought-iron ring near the top of one of the posts. Rapping his knuckles against the door, he waited until a gravelly voice answered, "Come on in. It ain't locked."

A bald-headed man who appeared to be in his early fifties glanced up from behind a small, scarred desk when Cody entered the jail. The man's blue eyes narrowed with a touch of suspicion as they took in the stranger crossing the threshold. The same gravelly voice that had bid Cody to enter asked, "How can I help you, neighbor?"

Slipping off his Stetson, Cody replied, "I'm looking for the local sheriff."

"You're lookin' at him—the only sheriff this town's had since people hereabout decided they had need of one." The man leaned back in his chair, his gaze still summing up the stranger while the fingers of his right hand toyed with the end of a mustache that was more salt than pepper. "Name's Howard Patterson. How can I help you?"

"I'm Sam Colton." The Ranger held out a hand.

Patterson pushed from his chair and took Cody's hand. The man's grip was surprising. There was a soft look to the lawman, and though Cody wouldn't describe Patterson as fat, his belly protruded over his belt. The white shirt and khaki breeches he wore were rumpled as though he had slept the night in them or didn't care about his appearance.

Patterson sank back into his chair and continued to stare at Cody. "Like I said, Mr. Colton, how can I help you?"

Cody assumed his ordered cover. "I'm with the Texas and Pacific—an investigator. I've been assigned to gather information on the recent train wreck here for an insurance report."

Even though he posed as the railroad's own brand of lawman, he'd be able to move more freely than if he had identified himself as a Texas Ranger. The status of Ranger carried a lot of weight in the state. Ranging companies had been born during the early days of American immigration into then-Mexican Texas, and their Indian-fighting ability had become legend. Reestablished after the Civil War, Texas Rangers had grown to legendary status among Texans. When a Ranger was assigned to a case, that case was expected to be solved—and fast.

The opposite side of the coin—and one that often hindered an investigation—was that lawbreakers threw up every guard they had when alerted to a Ranger's presence. Since Cody had to have a solid reason for being in Terrell without revealing his real identity— a stranger, a drifter asking questions, would arouse the suspicion of every man, woman, and child in no time—a railroad detective filled the bill.

"You're kinda like one of them Pinkerton boys, huh?" the sheriff asked, continuing to eye the Ranger.

"Not really," Cody replied. "I only get involved in matters that concern railroad security." He gestured toward the south. "I was surprised to see a train coming through here about an hour back. I was under the impression that the tracks were still torn up."

"Ain't nothin' shabby 'bout the crew sent in to clear things," Patterson answered. "Texas and Pacific had fifty men out from Fort Worth in a matter of hours after the wreck."

The lawman explained that less than a day had passed before the wreckage was cleared and the rails repaired. "Then they up and left—left the bodies to me and the cleanup work to a local crew. But they fixed them damned rails; the trains got to keep on schedule."

There was no mistaking the bitterness in Patterson's voice or the anger that darkened his face. It wasn't the cleanup work that was bothering the sheriff; Cody was sure of that. It was the bodies he had mentioned. A lawman in a farming community like Terrell was unaccustomed to having his routine disrupted in such a devastating way.

"But you ain't here about the cleanup, are you, Mr. Colton?" Patterson's blue eyes narrowed with suspicion again.

"No," Cody admitted. "As I said, I've been assigned to investigate the cause of the wreck and, if need be, aid in the apprehension of those responsible for it."

Patterson tented his fingers over his chest and glanced up at the ceiling. He heaved a sigh. "I was wonderin' how long it'd take the Texas and Pacific to get around to sendin' in a company snoop to make sure I was doin' my job." He looked back at Cody. "I don't appreciate that. This ain't no big city like Jefferson or Austin. I ain't got no army of deputies—just one man helpin' me. Things move at a different pace here, Mr. Colton, but they *do* get done in their own time."

Cody sensed that all that was needed was one wrong word on his part for him to become the focus of the frustration Patterson was experiencing over his inability to find the man or men who had caused the train wreck. And any headway he hoped to make required cooperation, not antagonism. Besides, he couldn't rule out the possibility that Patterson himself might be involved in the wreck. Like a man treading on thin ice, he used extreme caution.

"Sheriff Patterson, I wasn't sent here to do your job for you, but to provide what assistance I can. Matters like these can become mighty complicated for the railroad—things like insurance claims and lawsuits that can drag on for months, even years. I'm certain you can see why the Texas and Pacific would want a man of theirs involved in the investigation."

Something flashed in the sheriff's eyes, and Cody thought

it might be relief—like a drowning man tossed a line. The lawman's next words proved him totally wrong.

"Colton, I damned well know the smell of bullshit when it's in my nostrils, so let's get one thing straight between us: We both know you're here 'cause the Texas and Pacific don't think I can bring in whoever it was that sent their train flyin' off its tracks." The sheriff glared; the skin of his neck tinged red.

Patterson had hit on the truth—though it wasn't the Texas and Pacific that had sent him, and there'd be no way of convincing Patterson otherwise. Still, Cody wanted to avoid a straight-out head butting.

"If that's the way you want to see it, I can't do anything to change that. But the fact is both of us have a job to do that happens to be the same job. We can work together or go at it from different ends."

Patterson grunted, then muttered, "Fair enough."

Cody noted that the sheriff didn't mention which way he preferred to work—but it soon became clear. The only information Cody had about the train wreck was what he had garnered from a Jefferson newspaper editor and Major Jones's telegram. All of which amounted to nothing, except that a Texas and Pacific train had been wrecked by a person or persons unknown. And except to tally the dead at twenty, Patterson answered each of Cody's inquiries by saying, "You can read my reports—when I get 'em written."

After a half hour of verbal dead-ending, Cody gave up. "Would you at least point me in the direction of the wreck site?"

"Do better'n that." Patterson pulled a watch from a pocket and glanced at its face. "My deputy should be in here in another five minutes. I'll have him ride you out there."

Cody nodded. Patterson's concession was a small one, but it was better than nothing. Settling onto the only other chair in the office, Cody waited. The sheriff leaned back in his chair and stared up at the ceiling as though no one else were in the room with him.

•   •   •

"Didn't even remove the rails. Just pulled up the spikes. The weight of the engine hittin' them loose rails was all it took to send the whole train down the embankment. Never in all my life saw anythin' like it. Twenty people dead, their bodies all twisted and bleedin'. Seen Comanches hit two ranches out west, but bloody as that was, it weren't nothin' like this."

Cody listened as he rode westward along the railroad tracks beside Jeff Shiner. As tight-lipped as Howard Patterson was about the wreck, the twenty-five-year-old deputy seemed only too willing to provide whatever information he could . . . between his questions to Cody about life as a railroad detective. Cody's terse, improvised account of what it was like working for a railroad line didn't deter the deputy. With a youthful exuberance Shiner matched Cody's questions about the wreck one for one, inquiring into everything from job qualifications to the methods Cody intended to use in his investigation.

It soon became evident that Jeff's concept of a railroad detective came from reading too many lurid police magazines. Cody answered the questions as well as he could, doing his best to hide the fact he had no idea what he was talking about. Meanwhile he milked everything he could out of the deputy.

"That's the damnedest thing about all this," Jeff replied when asked about motives for the wreck. "There don't seem to be no reason for pullin' them spikes from the rails. There was a bank bag and two mail sacks on the train, but they weren't touched. Nothin' was taken. Don't make no sense at all, if you ask me."

"And you've no suspects?"

"Nobody even in mind. Whoever went after them spikes covered their tracks real good. Howard and me've ridden a five-mile circle about the wreck and couldn't pick up nothin' more'n a couple of tracks made by some ol' milk cows." Jeff pulled off a wide-brimmed hat and scratched at a full head of bright yellow-blond hair. "Hell, Indians don't even cover their tracks that good."

Indians don't go around wrecking trains, Cody thought as he explained to the deputy that he would start the investigation by questioning everyone who might know anything about the wreck.

"Anyway, I wouldn't go askin' Howard too many questions," the deputy advised with a chuckle. "From the look on his face when I walked into the office, I'd say he don't take too kindly to you bein' here."

"An understatement," Cody conceded dryly.

His presence in Terrell threatened the sheriff, no doubt about it. Howard Patterson was an aging man who in all likelihood was quite capable of handling the day-to-day problems of the small farming community. But no doubt he had grown complacent over the years, falling into the sleepy rhythm of his town.

The Texas and Pacific wreck had brought his world crashing down onto his shoulders. A train wreck was far beyond keeping rowdy farm boys in line on a Saturday night or tracking down an occasional stolen cow or horse. Patterson was in over his head, a conclusion made inescapable for him by Cody's arrival in town. The Ranger could only guess at Patterson's reaction were the lawman to know the intruding railroad detective's real identity.

"How long you been doin' railroad work?" Jeff asked as he tugged his hat back on.

"Since the end of the war," Cody replied.

The deputy whistled. "That's nigh over ten years. A man's got to be awful good at his work to keep a job that long."

Cody smiled but said nothing.

"Me, I guess I'm lucky to even have a job with this bum leg of mine." Jeff slapped a hand to his left thigh.

Cody had earlier noticed the deputy limping heavily on the leg, but it didn't seem to affect the way Jeff sat a saddle.

"Used to work west of Fort Worth on some of the ranches. Breakin' horses, mostly," Jeff explained. "Then a little over two years back I climbed atop a real mean bronc. After that mustang got through throwin' me, he went and did a fandango all over this leg. It ended up busted in four places. A couple of my pards set it, but their work weren't nothin' like what a doc could've done, and it healed crooked. It weren't much use for breakin' horses after that. Fortunately my pa had a cousin—third cousin actually—in the sheriffin' business. Howard didn't see how a gimpy leg would hurt none when it came to bein' a deputy, so he gave me this job.''

There was a touch of wistfulness in the young man's voice, as though he wished he were still working on a ranch but was resigned to his present lot in life. Cody glanced at the deputy's lame left leg. Even Jeff's canvas breeches couldn't disguise the unnatural bends in the limb.

Studying the young man from the corner of an eye as they continued the westward ride along the rails, Cody felt pity stirring in him. Blue-eyed, clean-shaven, blond, and handsome, Jeff Shiner was the image of what every father wished his son would mature to be. There was an element of tragedy in the crippling accident he had suffered.

On the other hand, put in another perspective, the young man was lucky. Similar accidents had left countless cowhands out in the cold, begging ranchers for the most menial of chores just to stay alive. Jeff was steadily employed and seemed able to handle the duties of his job.

"There it is," Jeff suddenly said, pointing. "Right there about a half mile ahead."

Cody wasn't certain what he expected to see. Shattered and twisted wreckage strewn along the railroad bed, he guessed. What he actually saw was ten men working around overturned cars. The scene appeared too clean to have claimed twenty lives, not at all like the sinking of the *Big Cypress Runner* with debris and cargo floating all over the river's surface.

They reached the wreck site, and when they dismounted, Jeff introduced Cody to a tall, slender man with a beard-stubbled face.

"This here's Will Vardeman, foreman of the crew. Mr. Colton's been assigned by the Texas and Pacific to help Howard and me investigate the wreck, Will."

"Mr. Colton." The crew foreman took the Ranger's hand in a viselike fist and shook it. "Anything me or the boys can do to help you, just let us know."

Cody perused the scene, then looked back at Vardeman. "I was expecting more damage."

"There was, before we got things cleaned up," the foreman answered. "One boxcar and one passenger car completely broke up when they left the track, and the engine and the rest of the cars flipped over and came to rest on their sides."

"The people who were killed, were they in the passenger car that broke?"

"Half of 'em," Jeff Shiner answered. "Would've thought all of 'em, from the looks of that car. Weren't a board in it that hadn't been splintered."

"We think we can salvage the engine and the rest of the cars," Vardeman said. "Mostly what we're doing now is waiting for the Texas and Pacific to send us a crane. When we get that, we'll right everything and see just how much damage there really is. An engine like that costs a powerful heap of money. If we can save it, there'll probably be a bonus in it for us."

With Jeff and Vardeman at his heels, Cody walked up the slight embankment and along the tracks. It took no genius to locate the place where the track had been tampered with. Aside from obviously new rails, the earth had been gouged deeply around the spot, marking where the engine and the cars it pulled had left the track.

"We found the spikes along the side of the bed," Jeff said, pointing to both sides of the embankment. "They'd just been tossed aside. Weren't no attempt to hide 'em."

"Engineer didn't have a chance," Vardeman said. "He couldn't tell the spikes had been pulled. The loose rails flew out from under the engine the moment its weight hit them."

The average farmer on the north-central Texas plains wasn't equipped to yank spikes from rail ties, Cody mused to himself before voicing the thought.

"Whoever did this had to have the right tools. Does the Texas and Pacific keep a store of tools in town?"

"We've got a shed near the station," Vardeman answered with a nod. "Keep our tools and handcart there."

"Is it kept locked?"

"Never had any reason to keep it locked. That is, up till this. I got a good, heavy padlock on it now."

Whoever had pulled the spikes had probably taken the needed tools from that shed, Cody decided. "Was anything missing from the shed?" he asked.

"Howard and me done thought of that," Jeff spoke up. "We had Will here check everythin' out. Not even a hammer was missin'."

" 'Fraid he's right, Mr. Colton." Vardeman nodded to confirm the deputy's words. "Wasn't a thing gone from the shed."

Which didn't eliminate the possibility that the Texas and Pacific's own tools had been used to wreck the train. But it did mean that if tools had been taken, the borrower had also had the intelligence to return them when he was done. That the shed hadn't been kept under lock and key made everyone in town and the surrounding area a suspect. Cody silently cursed; he wasn't narrowing the field at all.

The afternoon sun gradually crept toward the western horizon as Cody spent the remainder of the day examining the wreck site and questioning the men in Vardeman's crew. Neither provided one shred of evidence to proceed on. The Ranger told himself it didn't matter as he mounted the buckskin and rode back toward Terrell with Jeff Shiner. After all, this was his first day in town. He couldn't expect to have everything wrapped up in a few hours.

What he needed now was a good meal, a hot bath, and a long night's sleep in a real bed. Tomorrow would be a fresh day, and he'd be well rested and clear-headed. He had made a start; that was all he could expect.

He glanced over a shoulder, watching Vardeman and his men gather their tools and prepare to return to town. A twinge of doubt niggled at his brain. He tried to ignore it but couldn't shake the feeling that if Sheriff Patterson and his deputy had been unable to turn up anything in six days, his own presence here would do little to change that situation.

CHAPTER

7

"More coffee, Mr. Colton?"

Glancing up from the single sheet of newsprint that was Terrell's weekly newspaper, Cody smiled at the rotund, gray-haired widow whose boardinghouse he had been staying in for the past three days.

"Please," he replied.

"Black?" Mrs. Vera Farris asked as she refilled his cup.

Cody nodded, taking a sip as the woman settled in her own chair across the table. Mrs. Farris's other three boarders had long since left the breakfast table; all were members of Will Vardeman's cleanup crew.

"Another biscuit?" Mrs. Farris asked. "Still plenty of ham left. Shouldn't let it go to waste."

Cody repressed an amused smile. The widow's tone was that of a mother attempting to convince a child that he should clean his plate—rather superfluously, since Cody had already put away four fried eggs, a slab of ham, and three biscuits dripping with butter and blackberry jam.

"A couple of those biscuits with some ham in between would make nice sandwiches for later," she suggested.

"You know, you're absolutely right," Cody said, giving in. He wasn't certain where he'd be later, but carrying along the biscuits and ham would assure him of something to munch on when his stomach began to rumble.

"Didn't you say that you had been in Jefferson before coming here, Mr. Colton?'' Mrs. Farris asked as she assembled the sandwiches and wrapped them in a napkin.

''Yes. Why?''

''I was just noticing the headline there on the front page—about that riverboat explosion in Jefferson,'' she replied. ''Were you there when that happened?''

Cody flipped the paper over and glanced at the story that had pushed Terrell's own disaster off the front page.

''Yes, I was there. It was quite an awful sight.''

He considered mentioning he had been aboard the ill-fated stern-wheeler, then decided against it. The memories of that night—the nameless woman who had sacrificed her own life for that of a young boy—were too painfully close.

''The account here is very accurate,'' he added to head off any further questions about the riverboat explosion. ''You should read it.''

He returned to the newspaper, reading the back-page story about the Texas and Pacific wreck. It told him nothing that he didn't already know: The investigation was ongoing, and no suspect had been arrested in the case. Near the end of the account was a paragraph that named him as a detective brought into the investigation by the Texas and Pacific.

Farther down the page a smaller headline, placed near an advertisement for the local general store, drew his attention. The boldfaced head declared: STAGECOACH ROBBED! TWO WOMEN GUNNED DOWN!

The story briefly described a stagecoach robbery that had occurred nine days before near Texas's capital, Austin. Three masked highwaymen had stopped the coach, robbed all the travelers, then killed the two women passengers aboard the stage. The article proclaimed that the shooting had come ''without provocation'' and that the women had been coldly gunned down.

Cody scowled as he reread the story's dateline—the robbery had occurred on the same day the *Big Cypress Runner* had sunk and the train had been derailed. All in all the day had been a black one for the transportation industry within the Lone Star State.

Folding the single-sheet newspaper and stuffing it into a jacket pocket with the intention of reading the rest of the articles later, he took two quick sips from the coffee cup, then rose. He was wasting time. Three days had passed since his arrival in Terrell, and he was no closer to finding the answers he sought than when he had first ridden in. And he wasn't getting nearer his objective by letting the morning slip by while he perused week-old news stories.

"Will you be back in time for dinner, Mr. Colton?" Mrs. Farris asked. "I'll be serving chicken and dumplings."

"Unless something unexpected comes up, I'll be here."

Taking his Stetson from a hat rack near the door, Cody stepped out into a morning overcast with slate-gray clouds. Had he been anywhere but Texas, he'd have predicted rain before the day was out. But this *was* Texas, and this was summer. It would rain or it wouldn't; there was no outguessing Texas weather.

As Cody closed the white picket gate behind him, his answer to Mrs. Farris—*"Unless something unexpected comes up"*—echoed in his mind. He prayed that something unexpected *would* arise, but reason told him that this morning held no prospect of being any different from the first three mornings he had spent in Terrell. If anything, it might prove to be more useless.

During the previous three days, he had questioned everyone from the mayor to the blacksmith, hoping to find some thin thread that would eventually lead to the person who had loosened the section of railroad tracks. He had found absolutely nothing, and no one had the slightest inkling of who might be behind the wreck. After all, the consensus was, the railroad was good for the town. Business had doubled since the train had begun to run.

Cody started walking toward the center of town. Business might have been on the upswing in Terrell, but that didn't stop someone from pulling the spikes on a section of track and killing twenty people. And there was the possibility that, having succeeded once, that same person might do it again. Cody was here to make certain that that particular possibility wasn't realized.

Only he wasn't getting anywhere. He silently cursed as he mentally ran over all he had done since arriving in Terrell. He could recall no stone that he hadn't turned over—in several cases turned over twice. The truth was he had reached the end of his rope and had no idea where to turn next.

"Colton, hold up a minute!"

He halted, glancing to the left. Sheriff Howard Patterson stepped from the jail. The only good thing to come out of his failure in the investigation, Cody thought, was that Patterson no longer saw him as a threat. The lawman would never be described as friendly, but he had abandoned the tight-lipped stance he had taken the day Cody rode into town.

"Vera Farris must be feeding you well," Patterson said with a grin. "You're movin' late this mornin'."

"Trying to figure my options." Cody told himself the lawman's smile was an attempt at being congenial—yet he couldn't help seeing it as gloating over his inability to find some shred of evidence that would launch the case.

"And?" Patterson hiked an inquisitive eyebrow.

"I start again, from the beginning." Cody could think of no other course of action. "I backtrack—go over everything and see if I've overlooked anything. Anything at all."

"I've done that ten times now," the sheriff said sympathetically. "There ain't nothin' to find."

Cody admitted to himself that Patterson might be right. Unsolvable crimes were not a rarity. But Cody was stubborn. "Maybe so, but I'm not willing to give up just yet."

Patterson shrugged. "Where're you goin' to start?"

"I thought I'd ride back out to the wreck site."

A rumble of distant thunder briefly pulled the sheriff's attention to the clouds overhead. When he looked back at Cody, he said, "You'll have to ride out on your own. A couple of cows disappeared out of a barn last night. I had to send Jeff west of town to see if he could find somethin'."

"I can find my way," Cody said. "Just follow the tracks until I get there."

Patterson's mouth opened for a moment, like he wanted to say something more. Then it closed. He thumbed back his hat and glanced at the sky again. "Then you'd best be goin'. Looks like it might come a gully washer 'fore the day's out."

With a nod Cody turned from the lawman and retrieved his buckskin from the livery stable. He headed west, following the railroad tracks out of town. A humid stillness hung over the land. Now and then thunder rolled, but it remained distant, and Cody could discern no flashes of lightning among the clouds that blanketed the sky from horizon to horizon.

He was nearing the wreck site when Will Vardeman caught sight of him, raising an arm high and hailing him. Nudging the gelding with his spurs, Cody eased the horse into a loping gallop to cover the half mile separating him from the railroad crew.

"Missed you at breakfast," Vardeman said as Cody reined in. "I was going to invite you out to take a look-see at how things were coming along." He smiled. "Guess the invite wasn't necessary."

Cody glanced at the overturned engine and a single car—all that remained of the wreck. "Looks like you'll be through here soon."

"A day, two at the most if the bigwigs would send on that crane they promised over a week ago. Anything I can help you with today?"

Shaking his head, Cody replied. "No, I was just going to take another look around."

"Take your time." Vardeman waved an arm about him. "If you need any help, give a yell. Meanwhile, I've got to keep these boys busy. We'll get this car righted today, if the weather holds out." The foreman shot a dubious glance overhead when he turned and walked back to his crew.

Tugging on the buckskin's reins, Cody eased the horse up the railroad embankment, letting the animal pick its own way among the ties and gravel while he examined the area. What he expected to find he didn't know—but it made no matter since he didn't find it.

Moving down the embankment, he rode around the site three times in ever-widening circles. He remembered Jeff Shiner saying that he and the sheriff had scoured the surrounding countryside for tracks but had found none. Cody's short inspection brought the same results. Though, he reminded himself, if there had been any tracks to begin with, the work crew would have obliterated them long before.

Completing his third circuit of the area, he reined the gelding to the west, riding beside the rails. He still didn't expect to find anything, just wanted time to think through the puzzle surrounding him. He was certain the pieces were there; he just couldn't see them.

Someone had wrecked a train and killed twenty people in the process. But those he had questioned in town had no motive for causing the wreck. Everyone claimed that the coming of the Texas and Pacific was a financial boon.

Not for everyone, he thought. No matter what the townsfolk said, there had to be someone disgruntled with the railroad. This *was* Texas, after all. He had just been in the state's largest city, and the city fathers had slammed the door in Jay Gould's face. Not everyone viewed railroads as progress.

Someone in Terrell had a score to settle with the Texas and Pacific. But who? And why?

Why? The question nagged at him. He had been approaching the investigation from the wrong angle. Motive was what he should be searching for. Find that and the odds were he'd find the man who had wrecked the train.

And he couldn't rely on the present to provide that motive, he realized. Whoever had yanked those spikes might have been harboring a grudge against the Texas and Pacific for some time—a grudge that his neighbors had forgotten amid the prosperity the railroad had brought to Terrell.

That was the approach! He pulled the buckskin up, his gaze scanning the prairie around him. He'd have to pick Sheriff Patterson's and Jeff Shiner's brains to get what he wanted. A list of those who had opposed the railroad when construction had begun would give him something to work with. For the first time in three days Cody felt that he had found a crack in the wall that had been barricading his way.

Something in the distance caught the Ranger's eye. Peering intently, he focused on a long hill rising from the grasslands a quarter mile away. Railroad engineers had cut through the hill rather than laying their tracks on the contour of the land. But it wasn't the rails that drew his attention; it was a dark object standing on top of the treeless rise above the cut.

At first he thought it might be a man or an animal. Whatever it was, it didn't move. Cody tapped his spurs to the gelding's flanks, and the horse broke from an easy walk into a long-legged lope.

Cresting the hill, Cody halted his mount by what had drawn his gaze: a neatly stacked pile of logs, each five to six feet in length. He swung from the saddle and walked to the logs. A pair of wooden stakes had been driven into the ground on the railroad side of the pile to hold the logs in place. Two quick blows from a sledgehammer would easily dislodge the stakes and send the logs tumbling to the tracks below.

Cody's mouth felt suddenly dry. This was no innocent woodpile. It was another train wreck in the making.

The sap still seeping from the ends of the logs was all Cody needed to assure himself that the wood was fresh cut. He stood and scanned the terrain around the hill. A mile to the west he sighted a line of trees growing along a creek bed. In all likelihood the logs had been cut there and brought here.

A sharp crack sounded in the distance, and splintered bark and wood exploded from the logs at Cody's side. There was no mistaking the report of a rifle—or the effect of a slug. Cody dropped behind the logs. Someone was firing at him.

His right hand slipped to the holster on his hip and eased the .45-caliber Colt from leather. Thumbing back the hammer, Cody inched to the corner of the logs and peered to the west. Nothing. Pulling back, he crept to the opposite side of the stack. Still he saw nothing. Whoever was out there had a sea of high grass to hide in, while Cody was stuck on top of a hill—a sitting target.

The gelding stood thirty feet away to his left, grazing on the grass covering the rise. If the animal had been frightened by the rifle shot, it gave no indication of it. Cody glanced back to the prairie spread out below the hill. He still saw no sign of the gunman. His gaze darted to the buckskin again. He had to reach the horse and get off the rise. He rose to a crouch.

Another rifle report barked. Whining lead slammed into the logs, showering splinters into the air.

Shooting out from behind the pile, Cody covered the distance between him and the horse in bounding strides. Without pausing to snatch up the reins looped around the gelding's neck, he leapt into the saddle and slammed his spurs into the buckskin's flanks. The horse grunted and bolted forward while its rider scrambled for the reins.

A third shot resounded. A buzz like an angry hornet screamed by Cody's right ear as the bullet narrowly missed its intended target.

Halfway down the backside of the hill Cody pulled back on the reins, bringing his mount to an abrupt halt. He was out of range now; there was time to think.

The revolver in his hand was no match for a rifle. He shoved it back into the holster and freed the Winchester from its saddle boot. Whoever was taking potshots at him would surely expect him to be hightailing it back to town. But Cody had no intention of tucking his tail between his legs and running. Odds were that the man out there with his finger on the rifle trigger was the one who had brought the logs to the hilltop. And just as likely the rifleman had pulled the spikes on a section of rail.

Cody dismounted by a large rock in the grass and tied the buckskin's reins to it. The weight wouldn't stop the horse from running off if he took a mind to it, but it'd impede his wandering if he was set on grazing.

Running to the bottom of the hill, Cody circled to the north. In a crouch he eased around the hill's base enough to study the prairie to the west. Two hundred yards away stood a man, gazing at the rise—making sure his elusive target had definitely flown.

The Ranger smiled humorlessly. While the gunman was focused on the top of the slope, Cody planned to give him a little surprise. Dropping to hands and knees, he began to crawl forward through the waist-high grass. There was no possible way he could actually sneak up on the gunman, but with luck he'd get close enough to make the Winchester deadly effective.

Thunder boomed overhead. Cody glanced up, and a raindrop the size of a silver dollar smacked him directly between the eyes. There wasn't even time to blink the water away before the sky opened up and dumped a wall of chilling water. Lightning flashed from cloud to cloud, setting off another cannonade of thunder.

Rather than bemoaning the deluge, Cody used it to his advantage and scrambled forward. The heavy downpour would certainly blind the rifleman as much as it impaired his own vision, and the rumbling thunder would cover the noise he made as he pushed through the high grass.

He had covered about a hundred yards before he stopped and risked peering above the top of the grass. The gunman now sat mounted on a bay horse. Cody blinked a rivulet of water away from his eyes, then looked back to get a better look at rider and mount.

The rifleman was gone.

Cody's head snapped from one side to the other. Man and horse were nowhere to be seen. In literally the blink of an eye they were gone. But where to? And how?

Remaining in a crouch with the Winchester cocked and ready, the Ranger pressed forward. After covering fifty more yards he risked another glance around. Nothing. He cursed aloud as he stood upright. It made no sense. Men and horses didn't just up and disappear. They went somewhere.

Twenty rain-drenched yards farther he almost stumbled headfirst into that somewhere. A deeply eroded gulch, hidden by the dense grass, cut into the prairie. The rifleman had no doubt reined his mount into the gully and made his escape.

As to which way he had ridden, Cody could only guess. The storm's fury had begun to fill the bottom of the gulch with a minor river—more than enough water to cover the man's tracks.

Uncocking the Winchester, Cody swore. The unexpected he had wished for earlier had happened—for all the good it had done him. He turned and started back to the hill to find the buckskin and ride back into town. He was close to the answers he had come for; he could feel it. Why else would the gunman risk trying to kill him? But before he could join together all the pieces of the puzzle, he would need some help.

CHAPTER
8

Cody could almost see Howard Patterson's ears prick up the moment he mentioned the rifle shots. Until that point the sheriff had half listened to the Ranger's recounting of his morning activities, interspersing complaints about the water dripping from Cody's drenched clothing to puddle on the floor of the jail office.

"Shot at you?" The lawman's blue eyes narrowed as he ran a hand over his bald head. "You get a look at him?"

"Only from a distance." Cody tried to recall what details he could remember. "I couldn't swear to anything. I was never closer than a hundred yards, and the rain was coming down hard. He was riding a bay. That's about all I'm certain of. He disappeared in a gully. Runoff from the rain covered the gully's bottom by the time I reached it. I couldn't tell you which way he rode."

Patterson pursed his lips. "That ain't a lot to go on. If a man lined up all the saddle horses in this county, I'd bet half of 'em are bay. Hell, Jeff and I both ride bays. I can't go accusin' every man in town who owns a bay of wreckin' trains."

Cody sensed hesitancy in the lawman's tone. "I'm not asking you to do that. But I was damn close to the man we're after—so close that he tried to put three bullets in me. He knows he's failed. That's got to have him nervous enough to start making mistakes."

Patterson nodded thoughtfully. "What do you want to do next?"

"I'm not certain," Cody replied, shaking his head. He had thought about the next step all the way into town. "I think we should ride back to the hill. There might be something there that you'd find significant but that'd mean nothing to me. After that it wouldn't hurt to ride up and down the gully a few miles. We might be able to pick up our gunman's tracks."

Again Patterson pursed his lips. "Won't do no harm, I reckon." He glanced around the office. "Wish Jeff were back. Three men can cover a lot more ground than two when it comes to trackin'. But I guess there's no need waitin' for him. No tellin' when he'll make it back."

The sheriff pushed from his desk and glanced out the jail's single window. "Might as well take a slicker. It's still drizzlin' outside. Want one?"

Cody glanced at the soaking clothes plastered to his body. "I think it's a bit late," he said wryly.

Grinning, the sheriff took a yellow slicker from a coatrack near the door and pulled it on. "You might think about taking one of those." He indicated three scatterguns racked on the wall.

Cody shook his head. "I've got a Winchester on my saddle."

Patterson took a shotgun from the rack. "I prefer the double-barreled Greener. My eyes ain't what they were once. A shotgun's insurance that I hit what I'm aimin' for." He then lifted a box of shells from a shelf. "Doubt if I'll need these, but it wouldn't do to get caught short if somethin' comes up."

Cody silently agreed. He kept a box of cartridges for the Winchester in his saddlebags.

"Now"—Patterson opened the door to the jail—"let's take a look at them logs you found."

Patches of blue broke through the slate-gray clouds as Cody and Patterson urged their mounts up the grassy rise. The thunderstorm and the brief respite it brought from the summer heat had passed. Soon the unforgiving Texas sun would once again beat down, and the cooling rain would now serve only to make the remainder of the day unbearably humid.

At the hill's crest Cody remained in the saddle with his Winchester cocked and ready for the approach of any unwanted visitors while Sheriff Patterson dismounted the bay mare he rode and approached the chest-high pile of logs.

Patterson walked around the logs once before squatting first at one end of the pile and then the other. He reached out and ran his fingertips over the cut ends of the wood. "A crosscut saw was used on these."

"That mean anything?" Cody asked. He had noticed earlier that a saw had been used to cut the logs but had thought nothing of it.

"Could be." Patterson stood and stepped around the pile again. "Crosscut saws ain't unheard of in this country, but most farmers are more likely to stick with an ax. In case you haven't noticed, this here's prairie. Ain't that many trees growin' hereabouts. A man with a saw that can do this probably brought it with him from somewheres else."

"And you've got a man like that here?" Cody pressed, sensing Patterson had something to say but was reluctant to voice it.

"Most men in this country came from somewheres else," Patterson answered. "But only about ten of 'em might have a crosscut saw."

"And you've got one of those men in mind?" Cody's pulse doubled. Ten men narrowed the field to a manageable size.

"Could be," the sheriff said as he walked back to his horse and stepped into the saddle. "But I want to take a look at that gully before I start namin' names."

He lifted the braided reins from the bay's neck as though preparing to move out. But instead he glanced back at the pile of wood. "I will say one thing. You're right about them logs. A man could bring 'em down on the tracks with two swings of a sledgehammer. They're a train wreck just waitin' to happen, if I ever saw one."

Without another word Patterson clucked the bay forward. When he reached the gully, he reined toward the north. "We'll ride up this way for a couple of miles and see if we can pick up where that gunman of yours climbed up the bank."

"He might have ridden south," Cody suggested.

The sheriff nodded. "My bet is that's just what he did. That's why we're goin' north first—in case I'm wrong. If he went south, I've got a good idea where we'll find him."

Cody didn't understand the lawman's logic, but he didn't argue. With the Greener shotgun resting in the crook of his right arm and the way he sat straight in the saddle, his eyes darting over the prairie, Patterson had the look of a bloodhound with a fresh scent in his nostrils. If the sheriff was on the trail of the man they sought, then Cody didn't care what route he took—as long at it ended in the apprehension of whoever wrecked a train and murdered twenty people in the process.

They covered two miles to the north without any sign of a horse climbing the gully's banks. With an indecipherable grunt Patterson reined his mount around and began to retrace his path. He didn't stop until they reached the point where they had first approached the gully. There he turned to Cody.

"I guess I was just hopin' against hope," the lawman said as he looked southward along the muddy gully. " 'Cause I ain't got nothin' against Bill Quitman or any of his kin. The fact is, I like the man."

"Quitman?" Cody nudged back his Stetson and used a damp shirtsleeve to wipe at the sweat beaded on his brow.

"This here's a runoff gully. Ain't no water in it 'cept when we get a frog-strangler like we had this mornin'," Patterson replied, as though he hadn't heard Cody's question. "It feeds into that creek over yonder."

The sheriff pointed to the line of trees Cody had seen earlier.

"I suspect that's where the logs came from," the Ranger said.

"More'n likely," Patterson agreed with a nod. "Anyway, a little over a mile south of here, Bill Quitman's got a place.

You see, that creek's a good 'un. It don't run dry 'cept in the hottest of Augusts. That makes this prime land for a man tryin' to scratch out a livin' for his family from prairie dirt.''

He paused and looked back at Cody. "Even if there ain't enough rain for money crops, a man can haul water from that creek and keep his garden alive durin' dry spells. It won't put money in the bank, but it'll keep food in bellies. And that's damned important to a man with a family.''

Cody didn't need a lecture on the importance of water in Texas. He had been born here. Even the usually moist Piney Woods suffered in drought.

"You mentioned the name Bill Quitman twice now. Who is he?''

"He's the man who used to own all the land those Texas and Pacific rails you see are built on. At least a half-mile stretch of the railroad is on what used to be part of the Quitman place.''

Patterson explained that the state of Texas had owned none of the land in this portion of the plains that Jay Gould wished to build his railroad over. But when governments are involved and people want something that could line their pockets with money, there were always legal ways to obtain it. In this case that something was the farmland belonging to Bill Quitman.

"It didn't take no fancy legal maneuverin' or high-powered, expensive lawyers to do it, either,'' Patterson continued. "Seems like all any governmental body in this state has to do is determine that privately owned land would be better used for the 'general welfare of the public,' and they can get at that land. That's what all the towns and counties along the proposed Texas and Pacific route decided: that farmland would benefit the general welfare of the citizens if it were used for a rail line.''

Cody understood the situation. After all, he had just been in Jefferson where Jay Gould had attempted to convince the city council to give him free land to build his railroad on. Gould hadn't been as successful there as he had been here.

"The county commissioners met one day, and after a short public hearing they condemned all the land the Texas and

Pacific wanted for its rails,'' the sheriff said. ''Of course, they paid for the land. That's required by law. And they paid what's called fair market value. When it gets down to it, it means about a tenth of what the land is really worth, especially to a farmer.''

Patterson sighed, then continued, ''Quitman and some other farmers fought the condemnation proceedin' right up to the moment the county judge let his gavel fall. The rest of them farmers took the couple hundred dollars the county gave 'em and thought themselves lucky that they hadn't lost their entire farms. 'Course, most didn't lose as much as Bill Quitman. His place was a full section; now it's half that size.

''Anyway, as far as Quitman was concerned, seein' his land snatched away at a tenth of its value and then sold to the Texas and Pacific for ten acres on the penny was like wavin' a red flag in front of a bull. While the others gave up, he had just started to fight. He did it all legal. Hired himself a lawyer and went to court. Only thing, Bill Quitman ain't no rich man, and it'd take a man rich five times over to have enough money to stand up against the government and the Texas and Pacific. Inside a year, all Bill's money ran out. When he could no longer pay the attorney, there was no one to represent him in court. His case was thrown out.''

''And this Quitman hasn't given up his fight?'' Cody asked.

Patterson sadly shook his head. ''I hoped he had. But when he lost in court, he vowed that he'd make the railroad pay one way or the other for what they took from him. Bill Quitman ain't a man to make a vow lightly.'' The sheriff then added, ''Bill's wife died about eight months back. I thought it had taken the fight out of him. Haven't heard him say a thing against the railroad since he buried Sarah.''

''And all this time he's been stewing in his own hate,'' Cody said with an understanding nod.

''I ain't sayin' that's the way of it. But it don't take a college-educated man to see that's the way it might be.''

''And the crosscut saw. Is Quitman a man to keep such a tool?''

Patterson heaved another weary sigh and nodded. ''He and

his family came to this county right after the war. They were
from East Texas. He had helped run a lumber mill there with
his brother.''

Cody gazed southward along the gully. The water that had
rushed along its bottom but an hour ago was now rapidly
receding. "I think we'd better have a talk with this Bill Quitman. He sounds like he just might be the man we're looking
for.''

"Agreed," Patterson said. "But I'd appreciate it if you let
me do all the talkin'. Bill's a friend. If he's responsible for
the wreck, I'll know it . . . I'll know it.''

"It's your case, Sheriff," Cody noted. "I'm just here to
assist you.''

There was unspoken relief in the lawman's face when he
turned away and tapped his heels against the bay's sides.
"Come on. We ain't gettin' the job done sittin' here.''

Plowed fields, green with row upon row of maturing crops,
marked the Quitman farm's boundary, and a quarter mile beyond, Cody saw the barn and farmhouse. The house was that
strange blend of construction and materials common to the
Texas plains. One could almost read the history of the family
living inside by the structure of the house's parts.

From the side, the angle at which they approached, Cody
could see that the house's back room was made from simple
sod blocks. Green grass still grew on the roof. This had certainly been the Quitmans' original home. The second portion
of the house was constructed of sod and branches skillfully
woven together. The remaining section— four rooms from the
looks of it—were built of board, each one progressively cut
and planed with greater care and skill. The kitchen, with the
warm smell of baking corn-bread wafting from a stone chim-
ney, was built as a separate structure from the main house. A
shingle-roofed breezeway ran between house and kitchen.

As Cody studied the farmhouse, a woman wearing a man's
work shirt and breeches stepped from the kitchen. The afternoon breeze stirred strands of the raven hair that tumbled mid-

way down her back. She turned and stared at the approaching riders. It was difficult to discern the figure hidden by her choice of clothes, but Cody guessed she stood at least five feet seven in the boots she wore.

Cody smiled as he sensed interest stirring in him. His own height placed him taller than most men and towering above the majority of the members of the opposite sex. Height in a woman often caught his eye before he even noticed the beauty of her face. If there was anything that made him nervous around a woman, it was the feeling that if he touched her, she'd break and shatter like some porcelain doll.

"Charity Quitman," Patterson said softly as they drew closer to the farmhouse. "Don't let the name fool you. She's as pig-headed and stubborn as her pa, 'specially when it comes to the railroad." He grinned. "She ain't bad to look at, though."

When the two men halted their mounts, the young woman stepped from the breezeway and stuck a hand up to Patterson. "Sheriff. Wasn't expecting company today. What brings you out from town?"

Cody studied the woman's features. She was attractive, maybe even pretty with those big, dark eyes of hers—eyes as black as her cascading tresses. But he'd never describe her as beautiful. Her nose didn't seem to fit her face, though he couldn't put a finger on what it was about it that appeared out of place. And her mouth was a bit too large. But that didn't seem to matter when she smiled. The man's shirt and breeches she wore almost swallowed her up; yet, this close, they couldn't disguise the lithe, willowy figure beneath. He put her age somewhere near the midtwenties.

"This here's Sam Colton," the sheriff explained. The lawman nodded at his companion.

"Mr. Colton." Charity Quitman crossed to the Ranger and extended a hand.

"Miss Quitman." The strength of her grip surprised Cody.

"Charity, we need to talk with your pa," Patterson said. "Is he about?"

"Last time I saw him, he said something about going out

to the barn and shoeing one of the horses. If you two go fetch him, I'll put on some coffee. I've got some dewberry cobbler left from last night's supper to go with it.''

"No need to go to the bother,'' the sheriff said. "We'll just head over to the barn and talk with Bill.''

The young woman stood watching as the two men directed their mounts toward a two-story barn fifty yards to the left.

Patterson glanced at his companion. "Quite a young woman there. Works the fields as hard as a man when Bill needs her, and she can cook every bit as good as her momma did.''

Cody glanced back at the young woman. He had judged her too harshly. She was more than just attractive; definitely pretty. "I'd expect her to be married, raising a family of her own,'' he said.

"She was married, about two years back,'' Patterson explained. "To a fella named Jim White. Two months after they said their vows, Jim was out fishin' and a cottonmouth bit him. He was found dead halfway back to their house.''

"Then her name's White rather than Quitman,'' Cody said.

The sheriff shook his head. "She had it changed back to her maiden name. Paid five dollars to a lawyer to have it all done legal-like in district court. Don't think anybody knows why, but it gave everyone in town somethin' to talk about for a few weeks.''

Cody smiled. Anything even slightly out of the ordinary sent waves of gossip through a small community. He glanced over a shoulder again to watch Charity disappear into the house. It was strange some man hadn't snatched up such a good-looking young widow.

The metallic clink of a hammer on a horseshoe nail came from the open barn when they halted before it. Inside Cody saw a husky man securing a shoe to a gray mare's right forehoof. The man looked up when their shadows crossed the doorway. His eyes were as dark as his daughter's, but his thick, black hair was streaked with silver. Cody placed him in his late forties or early fifties. He didn't smile when his gaze alighted on the sheriff.

Patterson nodded a hello at the man. "Bill.''

"Howard." Bill Quitman twisted off the point of the nail protruding from the mare's hoof with the claw of the hammer. He then used a rasp to file it smooth against the hoof. He hit a couple of the other nails with the rasp before releasing the horse's leg and standing upright. Rubbing his lower back, he muttered, "I'm getting too old for smithing. Ought to let Melvin handle all the shoeing."

He cleaned his hands on a rag of burlap that dangled from a back pocket, then offered a hand to the lawman. "What can I help you with today, Howard?"

"This here's Sam Colton," Patterson said as Cody and Quitman shook hands. "He's with the railroad."

Bill Quitman's dark eyes narrowed. "Railroad?"

Cody remained silent as he had promised the sheriff he would.

"We need to ask you a few questions, Bill," Patterson said.

"About the wreck?" Quitman smiled humorlessly. "I was wondering how long it would take you to get around to me. Thought you'd be out here the day after that damned train jumped its tracks."

"Didn't have any need to, till today," the lawman said. "Today we found somethin' I didn't like, Bill. A stack of fresh-cut logs on a hill near the tracks about a mile from here. That hill used to be part of your land."

Cody glanced around the barn. Through the open door of a tack room, he glimpsed a saw hanging on the wall—a two-handled crosscut saw.

"No law against cutting logs in this country," Quitman said with a shrug. "Leastwise not that I know of."

"Them logs was stacked in such a way that they could be easily brought down on the tracks below," the sheriff continued. "It looked suspiciously like someone was considerin' usin' 'em to wreck another train."

"Wouldn't be a great loss, the way I see." Quitman's hands tightened to fists. "What are you getting at, Howard? You accusing me of wrecking that train?"

"Askin', Bill," Patterson replied.

Cody noticed the sheriff's own hands. Slowly, cautiously,

his right fingers rose so that their tips rested above the butt of the pistol holstered on his hip.

"Ask all you want." An odd little smile played across Quitman's mouth. "That doesn't mean I have to answer you."

"I wish you'd make this easy on the both of us," Patterson said. "I don't want to take you in, but if it comes to that, I will."

"Sounds like you already intend to do that, Howard—no matter what I say."

Cody frowned. Something wasn't right. Quitman was far too relaxed for a man about to be jailed for murdering twenty people. He studied him intently.

The sheriff shook his head. "It don't look good, Bill. Your hate for the Texas and Pacific is well known. You vowed to get back at the railroad for takin' your land." Patterson nodded toward the open tack room. "And that saw in there's just the kind used to cut them logs."

"I didn't cut the logs," Quitman replied, his tone too quick and light to suit Cody.

Patterson was silent for a moment, then said, "But I get the feelin' that you know who did it. Was it Charity? She might go along with you on somethin' like that. Or was it your son, Melvin?"

Cody's eyebrows rose. Quitman had mentioned a Melvin before, but the Ranger assumed he was a hired hand. He had been under the impression that Charity was the man's only child.

Quitman said nothing. He just stood and glared at the lawman.

Patterson sighed. "I was afraid of this. I think you'd better saddle up and come on back to town with us. After you've had yourself a sit in a cell for a while, you might decide—"

Patterson suddenly grunted. He staggered forward a step, his eyes rolling back in his head. Then he collapsed facedown on the barn floor.

Cody whipped around, his right hand going for the butt of the Colt, as a man's voice, seeping with satisfaction, declared, "You're not taking anybody anywhere!"

The revolver never cleared the holster. Cody found himself staring down the business end of a Sharps repeating rifle. A drop of blood clung to the dark muzzle that had just bludgeoned the back of Patterson's head. Behind that rifle stood a twenty-year-younger version of Bill Quitman. Melvin Quitman, Cody assumed. The farmer's son.

"Ease that Colt from the leather and drop it at your feet. Don't try to throw down on me. This Sharps'll open a nasty hole in you before your finger can find the trigger. Understand?" Melvin's tone left no doubt that he was capable of using the rifle if provoked—and Cody had no intention of provoking a man holding a rifle dead center on his chest.

"Understood." Using thumb and forefinger, he slipped the pistol from the holster and let it fall to the ground.

"Melvin, you had no need to go and—"

"Pa, there was no way you were going to talk yourself out of this," the younger Quitman said, cutting off his father. "You heard Howard. He was going to take you in. He'd already figured out that I cut the wood."

"Still . . ." Bill Quitman's voice trailed off as he stared down at the motionless lawman.

"We're still free, that's the only 'still' you have to think about," Melvin said. He jabbed Cody in the chest with the rifle. "Stranger, drag Howard into that tack room. You'll find some rope in the corner. Tie him up real good and tight."

Cody did as ordered, binding Patterson's wrists and ankles with a single length of rope.

"Now, you lay down on your stomach," Melvin commanded.

Cody did. With another length of rope Bill tied the Ranger's wrists behind his back, then bent Cody's legs back at the knees so that his hands and feet brushed each other. The older Quitman quickly and deftly hog-tied the wrists and ankles to one another. The joints of Cody's shoulder felt as though they'd be pulled apart.

"Stuff some rags in their mouths and lock them in," Melvin told his father.

Bill found some discarded burlap in a corner and fashioned two gags.

"That should keep them quiet," Melvin said as he waved his father from the tack room.

"What now?" Bill asked.

"We get their horses into the barn so that Charity doesn't notice them. No reason to get her involved in this," Melvin replied. "It'll be dark soon. Then we'll decide what to do with these two."

The door of the tack room closed. Cody heard a wooden pin being wedged into the latch, securing the door from the outside. Soon the sound of hooves told him that the Quitmans had brought his and Patterson's mounts into the barn. Then came the sound of the barn doors being shut and locked.

Cody listened to the retreating footfalls of the two men. His eyes then darted around the tack room, searching for something— anything!—he could use to cut through the ropes. Light still filtered through the cracks between the barn's walls, but as Melvin had said, it'd be dark soon. And Cody had no doubt what the Quitmans would decide to do with them. Though Cody had been born in Texas, he had no desire to be buried here—at least not today.

CHAPTER
9

Cody mumbled a string of unintelligible curses through his gag while he rocked belly down on the floor of the tack room. The fingers of his left hand strained to reach the taut ropes binding his ankles. Four times he pulled his knees back, attempting to press them flat against his thighs, and tried to hook the rope with his fingertips. Four times he failed. Another string of vehement curses sputtered incoherently from the gag.

If a man wanted to incapacitate someone, there was no more effective means than throwing him facedown on the ground, yanking his legs back, and hog-tying them to his wrists. The pressure from the limbs seeking to return to their natural positions kept the rope drawn tight, and the longer a man lay there, the more the circulation in his wrists was cut off. Sooner or later his fingers became all but useless, and there'd be no way he could get at the knots that held him. Usually.

Fortunately an active life had kept Cody's body flexible. The instant he had been certain Bill and Melvin Quitman were beyond earshot, he had managed to grasp the rope around his ankles and pull his legs down, creating enough slack that he could work at the knots. For a good hour he had been prying and digging his fingers into the tightly drawn hemp. A single knot had finally begun to loosen.

Suddenly his left hand gave out.

The rope slipped from his cramped fingers, and his legs jerked upright as they tried to straighten themselves. And the moment his legs snapped up, the rope tightened, pulling the loosened knot closed.

Cursing, he tried again to recapture the lost ankles with his right hand, failing four times. His arms and legs were unbearably cramped. But he couldn't give up and just lie there face to the floor. The Quitmans would be back; he was certain of that—and equally certain that he'd die at a far younger age than he'd always envisioned, if he was still trussed up when they returned.

A muffled groan drew his attention to the unconscious sheriff three feet to his left. Howard Patterson stirred. Or at least his arms and legs twitched, since the ropes holding him didn't leave much room for stirring. He moaned again. The sound was muffled by the gag in the lawman's mouth, but it was louder.

Cody felt more hopeful. A blow to the head, especially one that left a rifle barrel dripping with blood, was dangerous. More often than not it shattered the skull, driving bone fragments into the brain and usually resulting in death. If Patterson was waking, he was a lucky man.

It also meant there was a chance of getting out of the ropes.

Forgetting his own bindings for the moment, the Ranger rolled from side to side, inching his way over to the sheriff, then flopping onto a side. He scooted around until his bound ankles and the knots holding them were at Patterson's fingertips. For several seconds he chewed at the burlap gagging his mouth, compressing it with saliva.

"Howard, the ropes," he called out, his words muffled by the rough cloth so that they came out more like "Houare da opes." The sounds were close enough, and they weren't going to get any plainer. "Untie my ankles."

The sheriff mumbled something that Cody assumed translated to, "What ropes? What ankles?"

"*My* ankles!" Cody put as much sternness into his tone as the burlap allowed. "Hurry!"

Patterson half moaned and half mumbled more indecipherable syllables. Cody again tried to direct the lawman's hands to the ropes holding him but received the same lack of result for his efforts. Though conscious, Patterson was too groggy and dazed from the blow to his head to comprehend what was happening.

Cody scooted about on the floor until his fingers found the ropes binding the sheriff's hands and ankles. He had tied those ropes, sure, but untying them with his own hands bound was a different story. A full half hour passed before he managed to wedge a fingertip beneath a strand of rope and tug upward. Five more tugs and the first knot came free. Another quarter hour was required to untangle the second knot. He didn't have to worry about the third. Patterson, his senses fully returned now, jerked and tugged until he yanked his right wrist free.

The sheriff wrenched the gag from his mouth. "Damn! I didn't think you was ever goin' to get me out of that. Whoever tied them ropes did one hell of a job!"

Cody chose not to mention that he was the one responsible when the lawman yanked the gag from the Ranger's mouth. He then quickly untied the ropes binding Cody's wrists.

"What the hell happened?" Patterson asked his companion. "Where in hell are we? And how come my head feels like it's an overripe gourd about to explode?"

While Cody freed his ankles, he explained how they had gotten into their situation. It took more explaining than he reckoned. Patterson didn't even recall arriving at the Quitman farm. As the Ranger recounted everything that had occurred, the sheriff's eyes narrowed. He stood up, facing the wall of the barn, and the deep-yellow sunlight of late afternoon filtering a crack glinted cold and hard off the lawman's badge.

"Melvin?" Patterson spat out the name like a curse when Cody recounted how the younger Quitman had crept behind the sheriff and coldcocked him with a rifle barrel. "That son of a bitch will pay for this. Pay dearly." The sheriff gingerly probed the back of his head with three fingertips. "He raised a knot the size of a goose egg, and there's a scab as big as a silver dollar back here."

"Consider yourself lucky," Cody said, standing beside the sheriff. "You still have a head. But neither one of us will if those two come back and we're here."

The set of Patterson's face said more than words. If either or both Quitmans had been standing there, he'd have taken them on. Cody was glad he didn't have to face the lawman. Patterson would be a formidable opponent. Even with his paunchy beer belly he appeared quite capable of inflicting considerable damage if one got too close to his fists.

"Door's barred?" the sheriff asked as he tested it to answer his own question.

Both men leaned their shoulders against the wood. It didn't budge.

"A window in here's too much to ask for, I suppose," Patterson muttered, glancing around the tack room.

"Or our guns," Cody added, his own gaze moving over the walls to sort through the various tools hung on wooden pegs.

He found what he was looking for in a dim corner—an iron crowbar. Taking the bar from the wall, he walked about the room, testing the boards with his fingers.

"Wha'd'ya have in mind?" Patterson asked, hiking an eyebrow high over his right eye.

"If we can't open the door, I thought I'd make us a new one." Cody stepped to the far wall and pressed an eye against one of the larger cracks. He could see the Quitman house. No one moved outside it.

He didn't give the lawman the opportunity to ask for an explanation. Instead, he wedged an end of the bar into the crack and pulled it to one side. Wood groaned and creaked, and the board loosened. Shifting the bar lower, he repeated the process, and nails popped from support beams. The board was now free except for two nails holding it near the top of the wall.

"Two more of these and we'll be able to squeeze through," Cody announced.

"Are you crazy? Someone's goin' to hear all that racket!" Patterson peered out another crack and kept watch on the house.

When the lawman didn't report one of the Quitmans coming to investigate the sound, Cody attacked another board with the bar, then a third.

"Hold these up for me," he directed. "I'll slip outside, open the barn door, and let you out."

The sheriff pushed out on the three loose boards. Cody squatted and rolled through the opening. Once outside, he scrambled to his feet, swinging around to face the farmhouse. There was no sign of Bill, Melvin, or Charity.

Praying for his luck to hold out a bit longer, he ran to the front of the barn and lifted the board used to bar the double doors. He opened one of the doors just enough to duck inside and then unlocked the tack room.

Patterson stepped out. "Keep a watch on the house. I'll find our horses."

Cody moved back to the door, peering outside. All was quiet.

"They took our rifles, too," the sheriff remarked as he led the bay and the buckskin from their stalls. "About all we can do is mount up and ride like hell—and hope we can get out of range before Bill and Melvin notice us."

Cody would have preferred sneaking up on the house and taking the men here and now, but without pistol or rifle that'd be tantamount to suicide.

"Mount while I open the doors," he told the sheriff.

Patterson swung to his bay's back as the Ranger threw both barn doors wide. Grabbing the gelding's reins, he then leapt onto the buckskin. Both men slammed their spurs into their mounts' flanks and rode hell-for-leather toward Terrell. A full half mile lay between them and the Quitman farmhouse before Cody allowed himself to believe that they had managed to escape their captors.

Cody sat in Sheriff Howard Patterson's office, listening while the lawman rattled off a list of names to his deputy. Jeff Shiner responded to each with a nod of his head, then stepped toward the open door of the jail.

"And, Jeff," Patterson called to him, "tell all the men to carry pistols and rifles and ammunition for both. I don't want no trouble, but if it comes down to it, I want 'em ready."

Jeff nodded again and hurried into the night as fast as his crippled leg would allow.

Patterson watched the deputy depart; then, elbows resting on his age-scarred desk, his head drooped down and his eyes closed. After a moment he started massaging the back of his neck.

The blow that Melvin Quitman had inflicted was hurting Patterson. It didn't take a trained physician to see that. Cody walked to the desk and said, "Don't you think you should let a doctor take a look at your head?"

The sheriff glanced up, then opened a desk drawer to pull out a corked bottle of bourbon. "This town ain't big enough for a doctor. Got us a vet—but I ain't lettin' no horse doctor go pokin' 'round my head unless I'm on my deathbed." He held up the bottle. "This'll have to do."

He took a glass from the drawer, poured three fingers of the amber liquor, and downed it in two quick gulps. His pained expression said the medicinal alcohol wasn't of the highest quality. "Give it a minute or five to start workin', and I'll feel a mite better," he rasped. "Care for a shot?"

Cody lifted the bottle and took a whiff. He put it back on the desktop. "Think I'll pass."

Patterson smiled. "They don't pay a man enough 'round here to buy honest-to-God Kentucky bourbon. I have to make do with what Jess down at the saloon passes off as bourbon. It's got a jolt. For now that's enough."

Returning glass and bottle, Patterson closed the drawer and opened another. From this one he hefted two pistols. A Colt .44 he shoved into his empty holster; he passed an old Army Colt to Cody.

"It ain't much to look at by today's standards, but I modified it after the war. It'll take cartridges," Patterson said.

Cody balanced the weapon in his right hand. It was heavy and had enough kick to break a man's wrist when he fired it, if that man didn't know what he was doing. Cody did. He checked the cylinder. All chambers carried loads. He closed it with a metallic snap.

"Take these." The sheriff handed over two boxes of cartridges as Cody placed the old Colt in his holster. One of the boxes was for the pistol; the other was ammunition for the rifle the sheriff then took from the wall and gave the Ranger. Patterson took down another Greener scattergun for himself. ''Now all we do is wait for the others to get here.''

Settling into a chair to await the possemen Patterson had summoned, Cody watched the sheriff rest his head in his hands and once again close his eyes. There was no doubt that in spite of the healthy slug of whiskey he had downed, his head was pounding as if a demon with a sledgehammer had been turned loose inside.

Ten minutes passed before Jeff and two men appeared at the doorway to the jail. The deputy stepped inside. ''John and Ben Driggers ain't gonna make it. They're down in San Antonio, lookin' to buy some Mexican mustangs.''

Patterson lifted his head and opened his eyes. ''Don't matter none,'' he told the deputy. ''We still got ten men. That should be more'n needed to do the job.'' The sheriff's gaze shifted to Cody. ''Might as well mount up and wait in the saddle for the other men.''

Cody nodded, stood, and followed the lawmen outside to the horses. Another ten minutes passed before the last of the men the sheriff had called arrived. All carried rifles and pistols, as they had been instructed.

''Raise your right hands.'' Patterson waited until his summoned posse did as ordered. ''You men are hereby deputized for the time needed to apprehend and return Bill and Melvin Quitman to this jail. If the period of your service runs to more than two days, the county'll pay you a dollar a day for as long as I require your services.''

At the mention of the Quitmans a murmur of surprise rumbled through the posse. Patterson held up a hand to silence the men. When their eyes were on him, he explained all that had happened at the Quitman farm earlier.

''So, it appears we've found the men who wrecked that Texas and Pacific train—maybe stopped 'em from doin' it again,'' the sheriff said. ''I want these two alive, boys. I want 'em to stand trial. But if they decide to put up a fight, we'll take 'em any way that's necessary.''

The lawman didn't need to spell out that "necessary" included the possibility that the Quitmans might be brought back dead. Cody and the rest of the men understood that.

"We ain't gettin' the job done sittin' here," Patterson said. "Let's move out, and let's keep it quiet. Ain't no need to let Bill and Melvin know we're comin' till we get there."

CHAPTER
||||||||||||||||||||||| **10** |||||||||||||||||||||||

Light from a gibbous moon pushing above the eastern horizon bathed the north-central Texas prairie in a frosty glow. The silvery light invaded the stand of trees that the Quitman farmhouse stood in and washed across the front of the home. Patterson threw up an arm, bringing the posse to a halt a half mile from the house.

Cody studied the farmhouse. It appeared serene. Yellow lamplight filled two windows, and no shadows moved inside. It wasn't the picture he had expected. Bill and Melvin Quitman had certainly realized that their prisoners had escaped the moment the two lawmen's horses broke from the barn. Cody would've thought that the Quitmans would have their front porch barricaded and rifles poking out to greet any visitors.

"I don't like this," Patterson whispered. "It's too damned quiet. Makes me uncomfortable."

A whippoorwill's eerie cry sounded in the distance. Cody felt the men around him jerk upright in their saddles. They were more than edgy.

Sketching a circle in the air, Patterson instructed, "Spread out, boys. Surround the house. Keep your rifles ready, but don't fire until I give the signal. When y'all are in place, we'll move in slow and easy-like. There's only three of 'em. They can't cover us all at one time."

The mention of "three" caught the Ranger off guard. Cody had forgotten that the sheriff had said Charity Quitman was as much a fighter as her father. If it came down to gunplay, it was more than likely that the posse would face three rifles. Cody's chest felt hollow at the thought of Charity Quitman shouldering a rifle and firing on the men. That she could be cut down by a bullet—his bullet—bothered him.

Steeling himself to what had to be done, he recalled the wrecked Texas and Pacific train. Women had died because the Quitmans had pulled the spikes on a section of track.

A few seconds later Patterson told Cody and Jeff, "The boys are in position. Move in slow and quiet."

Signaling for the circle to close in, the sheriff clucked his bay forward at an easy walk. The posse responded; ten riders and their mounts slowly edged toward the farmhouse. When they were about two hundred yards from the front door, Patterson's right arm rose once again to signal a halt. The posse pulled up their mounts.

The sheriff, shotgun resting in the crook of his left arm, sat staring at the Quitman house for several long moments before he called, "Bill! Melvin! It's Howard Patterson! I got some boys out here with me, and we've got you surrounded! There ain't no way either of you is goin' to get away, so don't even think about it!"

He waited for an answer. None came. Cody still saw no movement in the house.

Patterson shouted again. "I don't want no trouble! The boys've got orders to keep their guns holstered unless either of you opens up! Now, I want you two to come on out to the porch with your hands high over your heads! Neither one of you'll be hurt! I promise you that! And I promise you that you'll get a fair trial!"

"More'n they gave them men and women on the train," Jeff Shiner grumbled.

Patterson shot a glance at his young deputy but said nothing. He turned back to the farmhouse. No one stepped outside or answered.

"Bill, Melvin, this ain't the time to be tryin' my patience, not after you tried to knock off my head this afternoon!" Patterson called out. "I want you two outside, and I want it now!"

"They ain't comin' out, Sheriff," a man to Cody's left said.

"Damn! I didn't want it to come to this." Patterson shook his head sadly, then turned back to the farmhouse. "I gave you two the chance to do this the right way, but now I'm goin' to count to ten, and if you ain't outside with your hands above your head, we're goin' to open up! I'm takin' you back to town one way or the other! The choice is yours! One . . . two . . . three . . ."

On the count of five Cody saw a shadow flicker across one of the windows as someone moved inside the house. His gaze darted to the front door. It didn't open.

". . . six . . . seven . . . eight . . . nine . . ." The lawman continued to count off the seconds.

The front door opened wide. A woman's voice came from within. "What are you hollering about out there?"

"Charity, this don't concern you none," Patterson answered. "I want your pa and brother, and I want 'em now. Time's up. Either they get outside, or me and the boys open up."

The dark-haired young woman stepped out onto the porch. The man's clothing she had worn earlier that day was gone, replaced by what appeared in the moonlight to be a white dress. "There's no need for guns, Howard Patterson. The only one you and your boys will be firing at is me."

"What?" Patterson's scowl was clearly visible in the moonlight.

"Why, Sheriff, have you been stricken deaf?" Charity answered, her voice brimming with sweetness and innocence. "I said that I was in here alone."

Cody frowned. No one, no matter how attractive she might be, had that much innocence in her voice unless she was up to something.

"You mean Bill and Melvin ain't hidin' inside?" the sheriff asked.

"That's exactly what I mean. They aren't here," Charity replied. "Both of them rode out just before sundown."

Right after Patterson and he had escaped from the barn, Cody thought. The Quitmans had known that Patterson would

return and bring a posse with him. They hadn't stuck around
to wait for their visitors.

"I'll have to come in and take a look for myself," the
sheriff said. "You understand that, don't you?"

"You're welcome to come in and do all the looking you
need," the young woman said cheerfully. "Spend the night if
you want. Pa's and Melvin's beds are empty."

"Ed," Patterson called to a man on his right, "you and
Charlie take a look in the barn. Jeff and I'll check out the
house."

"It could be a trick," Jeff warned. "She might be drawin'
us in close so's her pa and brother can get a clear bead on
us."

"Might be," Patterson agreed. "But I don't think Bill
would purposely put Charity in the line of fire. Most likely he
and Melvin lit out when they saw Cody and me hightailin' it
for town. Still, we have to check out the house." He paused,
then added, more to himself than aloud, "Don't know what
made me think they might be here. . . ."

Reining his horse forward, he didn't wait for the deputy to
respond. Cody and Jeff followed.

It took only a few minutes to search the house. As Charity
had said, it was empty. The two men who had checked the
barn reported the Quitmans' horses and tack were gone.

"What happened?" Patterson asked when he returned to
where Charity waited in the parlor.

"What do you think happened?" The sweet innocence had
disappeared from her voice. She had bought her father and
brother all the time that she could. There was no need to main-
tain a false front. "They did what any *sane* men would do if
a *crazy* old sheriff was trying to blame a train wreck on them:
They rode out of here."

"Which way did they head?" Cody asked.

Charity's dark eyes shot to him, flashing with anger, but she
didn't answer.

"Miss Quitman, it would make everything easier for your
father and brother and for us if you'd cooperate," Cody said.
"We've no intention of harming them."

"You've a strange sense of what's harmful, railroad man," Charity replied. "I've never seen a hangman's rope do anyone any good. That's what you've got in mind for Pa and Melvin—if you catch them."

Cody couldn't deny that. While he searched for the words to answer her, Patterson said to him, "We ain't goin' to get anythin' helpful out of her. Bill and Melvin are gone is all we need to know."

The sheriff stepped outside and called to the posse, "They ain't here, boys. Spread out and see if you can pick up their tracks. The sooner we can find 'em, the sooner we can bring 'em back."

"You aren't going to find them, Sheriff," Charity said, a smug smile on her face. "They've got hours on you."

Patterson shrugged. "Maybe, maybe not. But I reckon I'll try just the same."

Shouting outside drew Patterson back to the porch. Cody and Shiner were at his heels.

"Rich Bowman got their tracks, Sheriff," called a man riding a pinto as he drew up in front of the house. "They lit out to the south. Even in the moonlight you can see where their horses tromped down the grass. Ain't goin' to be hard to follow 'em at all."

"Then let's get on with it," Patterson ordered, waving Cody and the deputy back to their horses.

Cody mounted up, and as they rode out, he glanced over a shoulder. Charity Quitman stood silhouetted in the doorway to the house, watching them depart. The Ranger could easily imagine the hate in those coal-black eyes.

They rode silently; the idle talk among the men had faded by the end of the first hour. The only sounds that disturbed the prairie night were the rustle of the high grass as the horses plodded through it and the screech of an owl as it soared overhead in search of prey.

For two hours Cody kept alert in the saddle. Then the long, trying day took its toll. He started drifting in and out of sleep, nodding, then awakening when his chin dipped to his chest. Each time that occurred his head snapped up, and his eyes shot from one side to the other. He'd remain awake for another ten minutes, then drift again or jerk awake once more.

He reprimanded himself each time he awoke. He was on the trail of two men who had wrecked a train, taking the lives of twenty people. They were dangerous killers.

Nonetheless, he couldn't convince himself that there was any real peril. Charity Quitman had been right—her father and brother had far too much of a head start for the posse to ever catch up with them. Cody was certain that Mexico was where the two were headed. The best he or Patterson could hope for was that another lawman in south Texas might stumble on them before they reached the border. And that end would be better served back in Terrell at the telegraph office, wiring descriptions of the Quitmans to the cities and towns that lay on the southward route.

He glanced to his right as Patterson dug into a pocket and pulled out a watch. The sheriff thumbed it open and held it this way and that until its face caught the moonlight.

"What time is it?" Cody asked, wondering if the sheriff had also begun to realize the futility of tracking the Quitmans.

"Late." The word came as a noncommittal grunt. Patterson shifted his weight in the saddle while he scanned the prairie. "Reckon we should stick with this till mornin'. If we ain't caught sight of 'em by then, we'll turn back. I'll wire down to Waco, Austin, and San Antonio. Like as not somebody down south'll have a better chance of gettin' 'em'n we do."

Cody would've preferred reining around then and there, but he kept silent. He had held up his right hand with the others and was now legally a deputy sheriff and under Patterson's direct orders— as well as being a Ranger riding under Major John B. Jones's orders.

Not that there was any law that said a deputy couldn't resign. It was Jones and Ranger pride, not Patterson, that kept him riding. Cody decided to stick out the night on the slight possibility the Quitmans would be found. Odds were the major, when he was wired a report of what had happened, would order him into Mexico if that was what was needed to return the Quitmans. It wouldn't be the first time he had ridden below the border—but he preferred to stay north of the Rio Bravo.

"I make it to be twenty miles we've covered," Jeff Shiner said. "Horses need to take a breather or they'll play out on us."

Patterson gestured ahead. "Looks like a creek down yonder. We'll take a half hour's break there." He glanced over a shoulder at the men behind him, then added, "Most of the boys appear to be in need of a breather, too."

Cody's gaze shifted to the line of trees and brush that rose like a dark wall out of the prairie a mile ahead. There was no guarantee water ran in the stream that the vegetation marked, but the plan to rest the horses was a good one whether there was water or not. Both his and the sheriff's mounts had been going since morning. They'd soon be useless without a rest.

A murmur of approval ran through the men when Patterson turned and announced his plans for a break. Then the posse fell into silence again. Except for the soft rustle made by their passage, no sound reached Cody's ears for a half mile.

Then the neigh of a horse coming from the trees ahead cut through the night.

"Somebody's up there," Patterson said softly, easing back on his reins and halting the bay. "We're too far from anywhere for that to be a farm animal."

"Could be a stray that caught wind of our mounts," Jeff suggested.

"Could be," the sheriff agreed. "But I wouldn't give a copper for a man's life if he was fool enough to ride right up to that creek. My money says there's two rifles trained on us at this very moment and that those rifles belong to Bill and Melvin Quitman."

Shiner didn't respond; Cody found himself silently agreeing with the older lawman. Logic said that the Quitmans should be at least four hours ahead of them. But logic rarely came into play when dealing with criminal minds. The two men had probably thought themselves so distant from any pursuers that they decided to camp and rest for the night. If, Cody reminded himself, the horse ahead wasn't some stray run off from a farm.

Signaling the posse slowly forward, Patterson covered half the remaining ground to the trees before halting once again. He waved to the men behind him. They fanned out in a straight line to each side of the lawman. Patterson's thumb cocked the hammers of his double-barreled shotgun, a metallic clicking that was repeated all along the line of riders.

"Bill! Melvin!" the sheriff called. "I want you two to come out of them trees with your hands high! I'm too damned tired to talk it over! Either come out or me and the boys will open up!"

A blossom of yellow and blue flowered among the trees, and the sharp crack of a rifle report echoed in the night. The angry buzz of hot lead whined high over Cody's head.

"Down!" Patterson ordered. "Off them horses and get into the grass! Ed, Cal, take the mounts back out of range!"

Ten men scrambled from their saddles. Eight crouched or threw themselves belly down in the high grass while two gathered the reins of ten horses and made a hasty retreat northward, running until they were safely beyond rifle range.

Cody's eyes narrowed as his gaze probed the line of trees. He saw nothing. The foliage was too dense for the moonlight to penetrate. He wondered whether the prairie provided equal cover for him and the other possemen.

The shot had been purposely high—a warning that the posse was treading on dangerous ground. Or, Cody wondered, had it been a ruse to delay the posse while the two men mounted and rode hard for the south? He cocked his head from one side to the other, listening for hoofbeats. He heard nothing. The Quitmans remained in the trees. They had chosen this ground to make their stand.

"We still ain't certain that's Bill and Melvin," Patterson whispered. "But even if it ain't, whoever's in them trees ain't friendly. I want all you boys to lay one round into the high branches to make certain they know we're still here and mean business."

Eight men shouldered their rifles, waiting until the sheriff fired before squeezing the triggers of their own weapons. No answering fire came from the trees.

Again Cody strained to hear hoofbeats that'd signal a retreat by the Quitmans. He heard nothing.

"Bill," Patterson shouted, "you and your son are makin' a bad choice! There's still time to give yourselves up! You got my promise you won't be hurt and that you'll be given a fair trial!"

A hoarse, humorless laugh floated out of the trees. "Fair trial? How can we get a fair trial when you and the rest of the town're just looking for someone to hang that train wreck on, Howard? Hell, don't you realize that we know we're hanged men if we go and give ourselves up? If a man's gonna die, I reckon it makes no never mind whether it's back in Terrell with the whole town gawking or here and now . . . except here maybe we won't be the only ones who end up dead."

"Son of a bitch!" The curse came like a growl from Patterson's throat. "He ain't goin' to give up."

The sheriff glanced to each side of his position. "You boys, spread out a bit. Don't bunch up. You make too easy a target."

As the posse drifted out to each side of the lawman, Patterson called out again. "Bill, this ain't some game we're playin'! When we open up next time, we won't be firin' over your heads! Bein' cut down by lead ain't a pretty way to die!"

"Better than kickin' and squirmin' at the wrong end of a rope!" Bill Quitman answered, then punctuated his sentence with a rifle shot.

Unlike the first shot, this one sliced through the grass between Cody and the sheriff. This bullet wasn't meant to warn; it had been intended to kill.

"They can't see us no better than we can see them," Patterson told his men. "The only way those two'll be able to pin you down is by the flash of your shots. Fire, then roll. Don't stay put in one place for two shots. Understand?"

"Understood," repeated itself along the line of men.

"Good. Now, spread out far enough so when you roll, you won't end up where your neighbor was and take a slug meant for him. Empty your rifles into the trees, and then take a bead

on the fire that comes from their muzzles.'' His orders concluded, the lawman opened up with his shotgun, which was
totally useless as a distance weapon.

As was Patterson's approach to taking the men, Cody
thought. In spite of being outnumbered five to one, the Quitmans had the advantage because of the trees. All the fugitives
had to do was crouch behind a thick trunk and wait. Sooner
or later, by luck or skill, they'd begin picking off those in the
grass. Patterson was gambling that lucky shots would cut
down the two men before that happened—but luck was something Cody never relied on when it came to slugs.

When the posse opened up with their guns, he rolled back
a few yards, then in a low crouch moved to the right behind
the line of grass-concealed men. A hundred yards beyond the
last man, he cut southward, hidden by the high grass. His plan
was simple: Move in behind the father and son and take
them—alive if at all possible.

Reaching the line of trees, he leapt behind the trunk of an
ancient cottonwood and stood, back pressed to the rough bark.
He sucked down a steadying breath before inching around the
tree and peering toward the Quitmans' position. It was too
dark to make the men out.

Worse, he recognized, he hadn't considered a major flaw in
his plan, which was that to maneuver behind the Quitmans,
he had to place himself in the line of fire coming from the
posse. He had no desire to take a bullet from a foe, much less
from friends. Yet, if he wanted the Quitmans, he'd have to
risk the latter, like it or not.

Cocking his rifle, he pushed from the cottonwood and darted
beside an elm, then from the elm to a black willow that grew
beside a creek no more than three feet wide. Just as he started
to work along the water's edge toward where he hoped the
Quitmans hid, the rifle reports faded.

Bill Quitman shouted toward the posse, ''Now it's your turn
to dodge lead!''

The two men opened up, firing shot after shot into the prairie grass.

Though Cody still couldn't see the men, who were concealed from his line of sight by trees, he had no difficulty making out the blazes that burst from their muzzles. They were some fifty yards from where the Ranger stood. Using the echoing cracks of their own rifle fire to cover the sound of his movement, he hurried along the creek bank. Another massive black willow provided cover directly behind the twosome.

Now he could easily see both men, their sides awash in moonlight. They were crouched behind two cottonwoods about fifteen feet apart. No trees or bushes rose between Cody and the pair. It would be simple to cover each with the rifle. Leveling the muzzle of his weapon before him, the Ranger stepped from behind the willow.

And immediately leapt back behind it.

Having emptied their rifles, the Quitmans now ducked behind the cottonwoods to reload—and Patterson and the posse opened up again. Bullets whining like a swarm of angry bees flew into the trees, the random lead ripping into whatever stood in its path. Splintered bark showered the air, and twigs and minor limbs dropped from overhead. Cody pressed against the willow, drawing his arms in close to his body to protect them from a stray shot.

Finally the hail of bullets stopped. The instant the posse's volley ended, Cody once more stepped from behind the willow and swung his rifle around to cover the Quitmans. Before the twosome could begin yet another round of the deadly exchange, he ordered, "Put your guns down, and do it now. And don't try anything stupid like trying to throw down on me, 'cause you'll have a bullet through your head before your fingers can find the triggers."

Bill's and Melvin's heads slowly turned. Their gazes found Cody.

"Toss those rifles aside, and stand with your hands locked behind your necks," he commanded.

Father and son hesitated for the time needed to glance at each other. Bill nodded, wordlessly telling his son to comply. Both men threw their rifles to the ground and locked their hands behind their necks.

"Patterson!" Cody shouted. "Tell your men to put down

their guns! I've got Bill and Melvin, and they aren't going anywhere!''

Out on the prairie Cody saw nine men rise from the grass and cautiously walk toward the trees. The search for the men who had wrecked a Texas and Pacific train and killed twenty men and women was ended. All that remained was for the court to decide how to deal with them.

CHAPTER
11

The three-year-old boy wrapped his arms around Cody's neck and clung to him. Cody knew he was dreaming—it was the same dream that had haunted his sleep since that night on the Big Cypress Creek. He tried to wake himself, but the dream refused to depart. Though his brain struggled to deny the visions, there was no escaping the horrible scenes that his mind's eye relived. . . .

Leaving the unknown woman clinging to the wooden crate that bobbed in the inky water, Cody turned and began to swim for the bank. A piece of debris nudged his shoulder. He pushed it away and continued to swim. A water-soaked crate, more than half of it submerged, struck his shoulder. He edged to one side, dodging the flotsam.

The woman screamed. Twisting, he spun around in the river. A crate slammed into the woman's head. Her hands slipped from the wood she clung to, and she sank beneath the water, bubbles marking where she had been but a moment before.

"No!" he cried, his arms stretching out, reaching for her but finding only water. *"No!"*

Another crate slammed into his shoulder, and he batted it away—or tried to. The box shot toward him, again striking his shoulder. He shoved the container away a second time, but for a third time the box swept into his shoulder.

Part of Cody's mind rebelled as he nudged the crate away again. This hadn't been part of that night. Debris hadn't battered him while he was taking the boy to safety. But another box slid across the river and rammed into his shoulder. He thrust it away only to have yet another crate dig its edge into his shoulder.

This isn't right! This didn't happen! He shook his head, rejecting the distorted image of what had occurred. He had saved the boy, not been beaten to death by cargo spilled from the decks of the *Big Cypress Runner*. His eyes blinked open. Morning light, white and harsh, glared through an open window. He blinked again.

Something hard and cold nudged his left shoulder. He moaned; it prodded him again.

"Wha—?" Biting off his words, he came awake. He was staring directly into the dark muzzle of a pistol.

Slowly, cautiously, he lifted his gaze above the well of blue-black steel pointed between his eyes. Standing on the opposite end of the revolver was a young woman, dressed in a man's clothing. Her eyes were narrowed, and her lips were compressed into a determined line.

Cody immediately recognized the face. "Charity Quitman."

"Didn't know if you'd remember me or not." A dry sound something like a chuckle pushed from her throat. "But then, we *were* formally introduced."

"No need for formality," Cody replied. The words sounded silly as he uttered them, but they were all he could think of. His mind was still clogged with that damn dream. He needed time to clear it, time to decide how to deal with a pistol an inch from his forehead. He glanced at the open window. He didn't remember having opened it after returning from taking Bill and Melvin Quitman to Terrell's jail. No doubt Charity had used it to gain entrance to his room.

"I disagree," she said, shaking her head. "I'd prefer to keep this formal. As a matter of fact, I'd like to introduce Mr. Samuel Colt. He's with me to make certain that you act the perfect gentleman. After all, a young woman shouldn't be alone with a man without a chaperon."

"Actually, Mr. Colt and I have known each other for years," Cody said.

"Good. Then you're aware that I can take off the top of your skull with one shot from this."

The threat sounded deadly cold. Cody nodded.

"I also want you to know that that's what I'll do—or shoot off anything else that happens to be handy at the time—if you don't do exactly what I say, when I say it." She pressed the muzzle against his forehead to emphasize her point.

"Understood," Cody replied, though he wasn't certain the young woman had it in her to pull the trigger. "I'm at your command."

Easing back two steps, she motioned with the Colt. "I want you to get up and get dressed. We've business to attend to before this morning gets old."

The morning was already old to him. The posse and its prisoners hadn't returned to town until four A.M. It couldn't be later than eight now. "I'm in my all-togethers," he pointed out.

She shrugged. "I've seen a man buck naked before. And if you want to keep all together, get up and get dressed."

Cody sat up and slid his legs over the side of the bed. He looked at his pants, which were draped over a chair beside the bed. It was no time for modesty. Tossing the bedcovers aside, he stood.

Charity didn't blush—or even blink.

Cody did. His gun belt, which he had also hung over the chair was gone. For the first time he noticed it was his own pistol, the Army Colt that Patterson had loaned him last night, that the young woman held.

She waved the pistol to indicate he was to hurry. "Mr. Colt thinks it highly improper for a gentleman to stand around in front of a lady wearing nothing but his birthday suit."

"A lady wouldn't rouse a naked man from his bed with a cocked pistol," Cody muttered under his breath.

If Charity heard—or cared—she gave no indication. She simply stood there with the pistol leveled at him as he pulled on his trousers, then yanked on his socks and boots.

"What kind of business do you have in mind for us this morning?" he asked as he slipped into a shirt and buttoned it.

"I thought we'd go for a little stroll down the street and visit Howard Patterson," Charity answered, never taking her eyes off him. "You see, you're the key to unlocking a cell over at the jail."

"You intend to trade me for your father and brother?"

"That's the plan. I don't think the sheriff would want to see his railroad man filled with lead, do you?"

He wasn't certain how to answer that question. While the lawman and he were on speaking terms, Patterson just might consider Cody's death a fair trade for keeping the Quitmans behind bars.

"If you're set on working a trade," Cody said, "that means you want to be mighty careful with that old Colt. You wouldn't want it going off by accident or anything."

"I intend to be careful," Charity replied, smiling slightly. "But don't go getting the idea I won't use this pistol if you try anything stupid. Because I will. I have no use for a man who helped lock up my pa and brother for something they didn't do."

"If they're innocent, they sure have a strange way of displaying it." He told her about the logs piled by the railroad track and reminded her that the men of her family had assaulted Patterson and him, then left them hog-tied in the barn. "And they sure didn't act blameless when they opened fire on us last night. Fact is, they'd've killed every man in the posse if given the chance. Shooting at a posse isn't exactly the act of innocent men."

"It is if those men are about to be thrown in jail and then hung for something they didn't do," Charity retorted. "You know as well as I do that Pa and Melvin aren't going to get a fair trial in this town—not with every man, woman, and child in Terrell believing the railroad is God's own gift to Texans."

"I think you're wrong, but as long as you're holding that Colt, there's no sense trying to convince you." Cody started toward the door to the room. "If we're going to the jail, I guess we shouldn't delay it."

Charity hefted the pistol and pointed it at his head again.

"Not through the door. Use the window. I'm not about to alert everyone in this house that you're my hostage."

Cody turned to the window. "The window it is." The young woman had certainly planned this kidnapping step by step—including anticipating that he'd somehow try to alert the household as to what was happening. Though he wasn't at all fond of being the victim, he had to admire her resourcefulness.

"And, Mr. Colton," she said as Cody stuck a leg through the open window, "let me remind you that I *will* use this pistol if you try anything like making a break for it."

What he had in mind was taking the gun from her hand as she slipped out the window—but he wasn't given the opportunity. She had anticipated that, too, and somehow managed to duck outside without ever taking her eyes or the muzzle of the Colt off him.

"Now, turn around and start walking for the jail." She motioned with the Colt.

He did as ordered, and Charity was right behind him. The pistol's barrel pressed against the small of his back, feeling hard and cold.

On any given day a woman escorting a man down the main street of a small town at gunpoint would have gathered at least half that town's residents to see what was happening. Not this morning. Women carrying bundles in their arms, children playing with a wagon-wheel hoop, farmers driving their teams all passed Charity and Cody with no more than a nodded "good morning." Cody silently cursed the poor observational abilities of Terrell's citizens all the way to the jail's front door.

"Don't knock. Just open the door and go in," Charity ordered.

He did. Howard Patterson, who sat leaning back in the chair behind his desk, his head slumped as he napped, abruptly sat upright at the sound of their entry. A startled grunt burst from his lips.

"Colton? What's got you up so early this morning?" The sheriff blinked and rubbed at his eyes. "I was just waitin' for Jeff to come back to relieve me. Guess I drifted off for a piece there."

"I hope you're wide awake now"—Cody cocked his head at the woman behind him—" 'cause you've got a visitor. And she's not in a neighborly mood."

"Charity?" Patterson's eyes went wide and then narrowed as the woman stepped into view, closing the door behind her. "What in hell are you doin' here?"

"I've come to strike a bargain, Sheriff," she replied coolly. "A trade: this railroad man for my pa and brother."

"You ain't in much of a bargainin' position," Patterson said with a laugh, shaking his head.

"If you were standing in my boots, you'd have a different point of view," Cody said. "This young lady has your old Army Colt dug about an inch into my back."

"And I intend to use it," Charity added. "First on Colton here and then on you, if you don't hand over the keys to those cells." She prodded Cody forward to demonstrate she was truly holding a pistol on the Ranger.

"Charity, you're about to step into more trouble than you reckoned for," Patterson said. "Why don't you lay the gun aside and walk out of here?"

"I'm already in this all the way, Sheriff," she said. The young woman's dark eyes narrowed. "And forget about trying for your pistol. I can put a bullet in this railroad man before you can free that gun. In fact, you can pull the revolver from the holster—slowly— and toss it over in that corner."

Charity kept the old Army Colt pressed firmly into the small of Cody's back while the sheriff carefully eased the pistol from leather with forefinger and thumb and threw it into the corner.

"Now I want the keys to the cells, and I want you to get them slow and easy-like. Move too fast and I might get startled—and my finger would slip on the trigger," Charity warned.

There was no humor in her voice. She had come too far to back down now, and Cody realized that if necessary, she'd pull the trigger. He could only pray that Patterson didn't do anything that made it necessary.

"The keys are in the top drawer of my desk," the lawman said. "I'll have to open it."

"Then open it," Charity answered with a nod. "Just make certain all you bring out of that drawer is a ring of keys."

Steadily watching the young woman, Patterson opened the drawer. "They're right here," he said and reached inside to pull out a steel ring that had four oversized keys dangling from it. "Here they are. Do I bring 'em to you, or do you come and get 'em?"

Cody felt the pressure of the Colt's muzzle lessen as Charity pondered what step to take next. This was the moment he had hoped for. Spinning around, his arm slammed into her right wrist. The unexpected blow sent her hand to the right, away from his body. Startled, she yelped as her finger squeezed down on the trigger. The Colt barked, sounding like thunder within the confines of the small office as it fired harmlessly into the floor.

Cody clamped his hand around Charity's wrist, digging his thumbnail into the soft vulnerable underside and working back and forth. She cried out in pain and anger as her fingers splayed wide and dropped the Colt.

Ducking a left-handed blow that she swung wildly at his head, Cody spun the woman around and shoved her to the sheriff. "I believe she's yours now. We'll discuss the charges later."

Like a father snatching up a mischievous child, Patterson grabbed her by the back of the neck and pushed her toward the door that led to the cells. The two disappeared behind the door, and Cody heard the surprised voices of Bill and Melvin Quitman as the remaining member of their family was locked behind bars. A moment later the sheriff emerged. He looked at Cody and shook his head.

"I can't rightly say I like the women you've taken up with in this town," Patterson quipped dryly. He sank back behind his desk. "What kind of charges are you interested in pressin'?"

"None."

The sheriff's eyebrows rose.

"She did what anyone'd do if they found out their entire

family had been locked up. You can't fault her for that," Cody explained.

"I sure as hell can. We both might have been killed," Patterson replied. "But I won't charge her. I *do* want to give her time to cool down, though. Might keep her back there overnight to be on the safe side. That one's a wild heifer, if I ever saw one."

"There's no doubt about that." Cody smiled. "You also have to admit that it took a backbone like a steel rail to try what she did."

"I don't have to admit anythin'," Patterson said, snorting scornfully.

The Ranger's smile widened; then he said, "Well, I'll check in on you later and see how your three prisoners are coming along."

"Later?" The sheriff frowned. "Where're you goin'?"

"I was in the middle of catching up on a night's lost sleep. Don't see any reason not to give it another try." Cody turned and walked outside. In spite of the rubbery feel in his knees, he again found himself admiring Charity Quitman's grit. Women like her were a rarity. Not only was she quite a looker, she had more backbone than most men he knew.

Quite a looker—the words echoed in his head. He remembered Patterson using a similar phrase to describe her. He chuckled and told himself that Patterson was right. Charity Quitman *was* quite a looker.

CHAPTER
12

Cody opened the top three buttons of his shirt; then his hands dropped to his sides and he sighed. Regardless of the nagging aches that plagued his muscles and joints stemming from lack of sleep, he knew it would be useless to undress and climb back into the waiting bed.

He reached behind to the small of his back. He could still feel where Charity had pressed the muzzle of the Army Colt against his flesh. Little wonder that he couldn't sleep. Being dragged from slumber to find oneself staring down the barrel of a pistol was a sure way to get a man's heart racing and blood pumping through his veins.

He shook his head, then sat down at the small secretary placed opposite the bed. Opening the desk, he found a pen, inkwell, and white stationery neatly arranged within. He stared at the writing materials. Though the Quitmans—all three of them—sat safely in Howard Patterson's jail, one step remained before Cody's part in the investigation was completed, the one step he dreaded no matter what case he was on: writing a final report.

Cody stared at the ink, pen, and paper for several more moments before finally convincing himself that all he was doing was delaying the inevitable. The report had to be written. He pulled several sheets of paper from the tidy stack, lifted the pen, and dipped its nib into the black ink. After pondering his beginning line for a few additional minutes, he placed pen to paper and began to write.

• • •

Cody's head jerked up. He blinked, blinked again, then stared around. Several seconds of disorientation passed before he realized where he was. He glanced down at the three pages of the report he had completed. Two lines had been written at the top of a fourth.

So weariness had taken its toll after all, he thought, stretching. He vaguely recalled crossing his arms on the small desk and laying down his head, but he didn't remember falling asleep. He pulled out his pocket watch. Three P.M. He had slept at least four hours.

"Mr. Colton?" The widow Farris's voice outside the bedroom door was followed by a soft knock. "Mr. Colton, are you in there?"

Standing, Cody realized that Mrs. Farris's voice was what had awakened him. He walked to the door and opened it. "Hello, Mrs. Farris. How can I help you?"

"I'm sorry to disturb you," the woman said, a worried expression on her face, "but you've a visitor in the parlor."

"Visitor?" He frowned.

"Yes, and she insisted that she had to see you without delay. I told her you were probably resting, but that didn't matter to her."

"She?" Cody's frown deepened as he followed his landlady down a narrow, wood-paneled hallway.

Charity Quitman, still dressed in a man's shirt and breeches, sat demurely on a sofa with her hands folded in ladylike fashion on her lap. She stood up when he crossed the threshold. "Mr. Colton," she greeted him, a tentative smile on her face.

He stared at her, then asked, "Haven't we seen enough of each other for this day?"

The hopeful hint of a smile faded into disappointment. "I deserved that."

Cody shrugged. "I thought Sheriff Patterson intended to keep you locked up overnight to make sure you didn't try your hand on some other unwitting citizen. You don't happen to have another pistol hidden on you somewhere, do you?"

She looked down at the patterned throw rug beneath her

feet. "What I did this morning was wrong, but I didn't know what else to do."

"You might have tried hiring your father and brother an attorney rather than coming after me with a gun," the Ranger suggested. "If they're innocent, as you claim, they'll need a lawyer to handle their case when the district judge makes his circuit through town."

"They *are* innocent," her voice and eyes pleaded. "I swear, they had nothing to do with derailing the Texas and Pacific. Sure, we all hate the railroad for what it did to us, but none of us are murderers."

Cody refrained from mentioning that only a few hours earlier she had seemed prepared to carry through on a threat to blow off the top of his skull.

"They didn't do it, Mr. Cody," Charity continued. "They couldn't do anything that horrible. They couldn't! I know them. They would never hurt anyone unless there was a good reason."

"Most folks would say losing half of one's farm would be good reason. Your father did vow to get back at the railroad," Cody said.

"To get back at the Texas and Pacific in the courts, yes, but not kill people," she protested.

Again he restrained himself. Kinfolk of every man or woman accused of a crime throughout history had believed the members of their family innocent, no matter what the crime they were accused of.

"What about those logs I found near the tracks? That land used to belong to your father. Are you going to tell me that he or your brother didn't put them there?"

She shook her head. "No. Melvin stacked the logs there. But it wasn't to wreck another train."

Cody arched a skeptical eyebrow.

"I'm telling you the truth," she said. "Pa and Melvin use that hilltop to stack the logs they cut along that section of the streambed. Melvin was going to sell the wood to Harmon Woodall. Mr. Woodall has a farm about five miles north of that hill."

"Will this Woodall verify your brother cut the wood for him?" he asked.

Charity's eyes looked down again, and she shook her head. "It wasn't as if he hired Melvin to cut the wood. Melvin heard Harmon was going to build a new spring house and hoped to earn some extra money by selling him the logs."

Cody didn't believe the story. And he didn't expect a jury would place much weight in it either when Melvin Quitman took the stand to tell it. Melvin had positioned the wood too close to the tracks. He intended to use them to wreck another train; Cody was certain of that.

His gaze held Charity's when her eyes lifted. "Why are you telling me all this?"

She looked puzzled, as though she expected him to know the answer to his question. Finally she said, "The railroad pays you to do its investigating for them, don't they?"

"That's right," he confirmed with a nod.

"Then I want to hire you to work for me," she said. "I want you to prove Pa's and Melvin's innocence. My money's just as good as the Texas and Pacific's."

Cody couldn't hold back the amused chuckle that pushed from his throat.

Charity stared at him. "What's so funny? You're an investigator for hire, and I want to hire you."

Cody shook his head. Certainly she couldn't be as naive as she appeared.

"I asked you what's so funny?" she repeated sharply.

Realizing that the naiveté was no act, he answered gently, "Your offer. Even if I was at liberty to choose my own assignments, I'd have to refuse your offer. It'd be unethical for me to charge the Texas and Pacific for finding the men who wrecked one of their trains and then turn around and receive a fee for digging up evidence to prove those same two men innocent."

"But they *are* innocent," Charity protested. "There would be no conflict. You haven't found the men who wrecked that train. You would be—"

Cody held up a hand to stop her. "Last night I captured the

two men I believe wrecked the train. My job here in Terrell is through. If this is all you came here to discuss, I'm afraid you've wasted your time, Miss Quitman. If you feel you have any evidence that could prove the innocence of your father and brother, you should present it to Sheriff Patterson. The matter is totally in his hands now. As I said, my job here is completed.''

His tone was colder and more formal than he would have preferred. But he couldn't lie. He *had* done his job; the fate of Bill and Melvin Quitman now lay in the hands of a jury selected to hear their case.

"Patterson?" Skepticism left her lower jaw sagging. "You can't be serious. I think that you're a reasonably intelligent man, Mr. Colton. You know Howard Patterson fairly well by now. Do you honestly believe he gives a damn whether Pa and Melvin actually wrecked that train? All that matters to him is that he has two men he can march to the gallows. That's all he needs to get himself elected again.''

Cody sympathized with her position. The first day he had arrived in Terrell he had recognized that Howard Patterson was in over his head when it came to investigating the wreck. But it wasn't Patterson who had brought in the Quitmans; he had. And as far as he was concerned, the pair had done everything but sign a confession when they attacked the sheriff and him yesterday. That the two men had fled their home and then shot it out with the posse last night only solidified his conviction that the Quitmans were the men he sought.

"I'm sorry, but there's nothing I can do to help you," he said. "Take the advice I gave earlier: Hire an attorney for your father and brother.''

"And I'd like to tell you what you can do with your advice!" she snapped, anger flaming in her dark eyes. "I hoped you might be different, but you aren't. You and Howard Patterson are the same. You don't give a damn about finding out who really wrecked that train. All you want is a scapegoat—someone to take the blame so you can say you've done your job!''

"Miss Quitman—''

She didn't give him the chance to say anything more. Tears streaming down her cheeks, she stormed from the parlor and raced out of the boardinghouse, slamming the front door behind her so hard that the glass panes rattled.

The irrational urge to run after her and tell her that he'd accept her offer swelled within Cody. But he resisted. To become entangled in her problems would present a stickier quandary than a black widow's web. He had work to finish in the south. A certain Mexican rustler had been allowed to roam free for too long.

Still, he couldn't dispel the sight of Charity with tears streaming down her cheeks.

Cody pushed the image from his mind. It would lead nowhere. With a final glance over a shoulder at the front door, he turned and walked back to his room. He had a report to finish.

"What's this?" Howard Patterson suspiciously eyed the six-page report that Cody had placed on his desk.

"I'd like you to read that over, make certain I haven't left anything out, then sign on the last page to verify it," Cody said. "It's my report to Major John B. Jones in San Antonio. I'd like to put it in the mail tomorrow before I head back east."

Patterson's head jerked up and he stared at Cody. "San Antonio? Major John Jones? What the hell are you talkin' about, Colton? Major Jones is a bigwig in the Texas Rangers. Why would you be reportin' to him?"

"The name's Cody, not Colton." Cody pulled out his pocket watch, opened its hidden compartment, extracted the badge inside, and pinned it to his vest. "Don't reckon there's any need to keep this from you anymore, now that we've brought the Quitmans in."

"A Ranger?" Patterson continued to stare at Cody with his mouth hanging open. "I'll be damned!" he finally said after a full ten seconds had passed. "You're a Texas Ranger! You ain't working for the railroad!"

"Major Jones thought the sudden appearance of a Ranger in Terrell would cause too much commotion and had me pose as a railroad detective." Cody pointed to the report. "I still need for you to sign that. Then I can start back to San Antonio."

The sheriff looked at the handwritten pages and then back at the Ranger. "You won't be goin' anywhere tomorrow or maybe the next day, either. Not till you provide me with a notarized, witnessed statement."

"Statement?" It was Cody's turn to stare, uncertain what Patterson meant.

"An affidavit that can be introduced as evidence in the Quitmans' trial," Patterson answered. "Of course, if you don't want to go to all that trouble, you can stick around for three weeks. The district judge should be through about then, and you can take the stand and testify at the trial in person."

Cody hadn't considered that his testimony might be needed at the trial. The prospect of being stranded in Terrell until a jury heard his testimony hardly appealed to him. "Like I said, read over that report. If it's sufficient, I'll make a copy tonight and add some legal language here and there. Tomorrow morning you can drum up a notary and witnesses, and I'll sign it in their presence."

"Fair enough," the sheriff said, nodding. He leaned back in his chair and devoted his attention to the report.

Cody walked over to the office's other chair and settled into it, slipping his watch back in his breeches pocket. Inside the pocket he discovered the folded newspaper he had placed there yesterday morning and pulled it out. He scanned the front page, recalling the articles about the *Big Cypress Runner*'s sinking and the stagecoach robbery near Austin in which two women passengers had been gunned down by highwaymen, then turned the single-sheet paper over and found the article on the train wreck.

Details of the derailment were skimpy, padded with purple prose rather than fact. He found nothing that went beyond what he already knew. His gaze went down to the bottom of the page and a boxed, two-column list of those who had died in the wreck. Some of the names had bits of information beside them, such as ages and hometowns. The majority were simply names.

Cody's eyes scanned the two columns. Then the Ranger abruptly reread the list, having an inkling that there was something familiar about a name he had casually passed over the first time. He perused the list three more times but couldn't find the name that had caught his eye. Irritation niggled within him, the kind elicited by reading a memorable quote in a book that then can't be found again without rereading an entire chapter. Determined to locate that elusive name, he once more moved to the top of the list and read each individual name, more carefully this time.

He found what he was looking for two-thirds down the second column: Mrs. Mary Brady. It took several seconds of delving in his memory to recall why that name stood out. A Mary Brady, Mrs. Calvin Brady, had been Sheriff Manly Howell's missing passenger back in Jefferson— the woman who had purchased a berth aboard the *Big Cypress Runner*, but who no one among the crew or staff could remember boarding.

"Who is this Mrs. Mary Brady?" Cody asked, looking at Patterson.

"What?" The sheriff set aside the third page of the report.

"A Mrs. Mary Brady is listed here among those killed in the train wreck. Who is she?" Cody asked.

"Trouble spelled in capital letters," the lawman replied. "She was the wife of State Senator Calvin Brady. Brady's one of the more powerful men in Texas right now. Lot of folks say he'll be our next governor."

Cody drew in a breath. The lawman had just described the Mary Brady who was missing from the *Big Cypress Runner*. "Did she die in the derailment?"

Patterson gave him a look as though the Ranger was a complete idiot. "What d'ya mean, did she die? She's listed there among the twenty dead, ain't she? She was found near one of the overturned passenger cars. Apparently thrown through a window. Her neck was broken."

"And her body?" Cody asked. "What happened to her body?"

"It was shipped back to her husband, of course." Patterson's expression changed to that of a man who had just discovered he was alone in a room with a dangerous lunatic. "I reckon her husband buried her after that. That's what usually happens to the dead. You get a preacher to say some words over 'em, and you put 'em in the ground."

"Did Brady come to Terrell to identify the body?" A worm ate at Cody's brain. He didn't like the dark, dirty feel of it.

The sheriff shook his head. "No need. There was a conductor and passengers to identify her. Why? Did you know her—or Brady?"

"No." Cody glanced back at the newspaper's front page. The headlines about the riverboat sinking and the stagecoach murders jumped out at him.

"Then why're you so interested?" the sheriff pressed.

"I don't know." The Ranger sucked at his teeth. "I've got an uneasy feeling, but I'm not sure what's causing it."

Patterson shrugged and went back to reading the report. "This is pretty accurate," he announced. "Where do you want me to sign it?"

"At the bottom. I drew in two lines for your name and the date." Cody gave the lawman a glance, but his mind was elsewhere, attempting to capture that squirming worm of doubt that drilled into his mind.

"Yeah," the sheriff said. "I think this'll do good. Make me a copy, and add that legal language like you said, and it'll be perfect for the judge."

Cody nodded absently. "I'll do that."

Truth was, he had barely heard Patterson. He rose, collected the report, and walked from the office without a word. He hoped that the murky thought gathering in his mind was wrong—and there was only one way to prove or disprove it.

His stride quickened as he neared the telegraph office. He needed to send several wires before it closed.

CHAPTER
||||||||||||||||||||||||||||||| **13** |||||||||||||||||||||||||||||||

The wait for replies to the telegrams Cody had sent stretched from twenty-four hours to forty-eight, then to three days. The information he had requested from Jefferson sheriff Manly Howell finally came over the wire shortly before noon of that third day. Cody quickly scanned the yellow sheet of paper to get the gist of the East Texas lawman's answer, then carefully reread the telegram word for word.

The first sentence confirmed what Cody already knew: Neither Mary Brady's body nor any trace of the woman's having been on the *Big Cypress Runner* had been found. To Howell the senator's wife remained an unsolved mystery. The Ranger made a mental note to wire the sheriff, informing him of Mrs. Brady's death in the train derailment.

The next two brief sentences contained the information Cody had hoped for: Mary Brady had been booked on the *Big Cypress Runner* all the way to New Orleans, and from there her travel arrangements included passage up the Mississippi to St. Louis.

Folding the wire, Cody placed it in a vest pocket. This was a beginning; now all he had to do was wait for the other answers to come in.

The second telegram arrived by messenger while he was eating lunch at Mrs. Farris's boardinghouse. The Texas and Pacific confirmed what he had begun to suspect: Travel arrangements had been made through one of their offices for Mrs. Brady. Her itinerary had been to journey by train to the railhead in East Texas, where a private coach had been arranged to take her across Louisiana to the Mississippi River. As with her New Orleans plans she was to have traveled upriver via riverboat to St. Louis.

Cody folded the second message and placed it in his vest with the first.

He was in the middle of complimenting Mrs. Farris on the spicy prairie stew and the green-grape cobbler she had served for lunch when a knock sounded on the front door. It was a messenger from the telegraph office with the reply to the third wire Cody had sent three days before.

This message—a relatively long one—was from Ranger headquarters. The first portion provided the background on Texas State Senator Calvin Brady that Cody had requested. It basically repeated what the Ranger had already learned, using terms like "meteoric" to describe Brady's political rise in power. The biographical sketch portrayed the senator as a staunch supporter of states' rights and a man who appeared to have no political ambitions outside the state and didn't display any regard for national politics except where Texas and its interests, as Brady viewed them, were concerned.

There were no obvious black marks against the senator in the whole report. But the overall impression left by the sketch was that Brady applied the same techniques to his political life as he had in carving a ranching empire for himself out of the West Texas plains: He was willing to do what was needed to assure he succeeded in the endeavors he undertook. Though there was no indication that Brady had ever broken the law to achieve those ends, Cody assumed that, like other powerful men, the senator wasn't above bending the law when it proved profitable or expedient.

The second portion of the telegram was a single, short paragraph. It confirmed that Mary Brady had purchased a ticket aboard the stagecoach that had been robbed near Austin and again that she had made overland travel arrangements leading up the Mississippi to St. Louis.

Why would the wife of a prominent Texas state senator make three separate traveling plans that all eventually ended in St. Louis? Why would anyone make such extensive arrangements?

Cody shook his head as he placed the third wire in his vest pocket with the others. He could think of no ordinary person who'd go to the effort Mary Brady had to make certain she arrived at her destination, no matter what route she took. But fugitives attempting to confuse lawmen on their trail might go to such lengths. . . .

He made a mental note to check out any illegal activities the woman might have been involved in. If she were playing a shady hand, an influential man such as Calvin Brady surely had enough clout to see that a lid was kept on the situation and no mention was made of it in the newspapers.

Newspapers. An unconsidered possibility took root in the Ranger's mind. Giving his landlady a quick compliment on her lunch, Cody left the boardinghouse, mulling over the information he had just received.

A politician might go through such convoluted gyrations to hide the travel route he planned. That would imply political scandal and an attempt to avoid contact with reporters who smelled a hot story.

Cody mentally shook his head. He preferred the first possibility. After all, Mary Brady wasn't involved in politics; her husband was. If Calvin Brady had stepped into a scandal, the newspapers would be filled with the story, and there'd be no talk of his winning the governor's seat in the next election.

And that scandal might involve the senator's wife.

Maybe Mary Brady had been trying to avoid running into newspapermen. If so, that would also mean that—

Cody shoved the "ifs" from his mind. The more he considered Mary Brady being involved in a scandal, the more complicated his reasoning became. He needed to pare down his thinking.

Why had disaster struck the very riverboat, stagecoach, and train that Mary Brady had been booked on exactly the same day? Cody didn't believe in coincidence. That left only one answer: Someone other than the law had tried to stop her from leaving the state.

Another unanswered question reared its ugly head: Who?

He sensed he had begun to cut to the heart of the problem—but the solution had been hidden beneath layer upon layer of subterfuge by someone wanting to make certain that the truth never saw the light of day.

Who, dammit? he asked himself. He didn't know. And he didn't have one clue to point the way. But he did have a gut feeling that all he had done until this very moment was wander blindly around in a smoke screen that had been lit by Mary Brady's killer.

And as certain as he was of that, he was now equally certain that Bill and Melvin Quitman weren't responsible for the train wreck.

Like a sleepwalker suddenly shocked awake, Cody came to a dead stop on Terrell's main street. He had helped jail the wrong men! His face flushed with guilt, and his stomach gave a sickly churn. In spite of the circumstantial evidence, in spite of their own actions, Charity Quitman was right; her father and brother were innocent.

Cody looked around. Howard Patterson's jail stood directly across the street. He turned and raced into the sheriff's office.

Patterson, who was nursing a tin cup of coffee, looked up with mild surprise. "For a man who said he had business elsewheres, you sure are hangin' around for a long time."

"And a good afternoon to you, too," Cody said, then nodded a greeting to Jeff Shiner, who sat near the sheriff's desk.

Patterson glowered with disgust. "Ain't nothin' good about it. I got two murderers back there in a cell who need tryin', but they ain't goin' to be for at least another month 'cause the district judge up and died of a heart attack yesterday, and there won't be another appointed for at least a month. Atop that, I just had to toss Billy Jack Younger and Clinton Goggins in separate cells 'cause they was goin' at it over the Pirkle girl. And Jeff just rode in to say Trent Shirley's missin' ten head of beeves, and there ain't no sign of who made off with 'em or where the hell they went." Snorting angrily, he took another swig from the cup. He then looked back at the Ranger. "Just why *are* you still in town, Cody?"

"I had a few questions I wanted answered before I headed south." He reached into the vest pocket and retrieved the three telegrams. "I got the answers today. You might be interested in seeing them." He dropped the folded yellow sheets onto the lawman's desk.

Patterson lifted each of the telegrams and read them silently, then remarked, "I don't see how this rightly concerns me. What kind of travel arrangements Mary Brady made and where she was goin' really ain't got a hill of beans to do with two men wreckin' a train outside of my town."

It was clear that Patterson wanted a nice, unambiguous, *solved* case. These telegrams said they hadn't begun to unravel a crime that covered half of Texas.

Cody couldn't keep the sarcasm out of his voice when he asked, "Doesn't it strike you kind of odd that Mary Brady was booked on a stagecoach, a train, and a riverboat that all met with disaster the same day?"

"Odd, yes. But that riverboat and stage ain't no concern of mine. They didn't happen here. They're another sheriff's problem. I don't go stickin' this nose in other folks' problems unless I'm asked."

Jeff pulled the telegrams across the desk and read them as Cody said, "Sheriff, I know you aren't blind. Are you telling me that you can't see that the riverboat sinking, the stagecoach robbery and murders, and the train wreck are related?"

"Sounds like you're makin' out like you don't think the Quitmans wrecked that train no more," Jeff said, shoving the three telegrams back to the center of the desk.

"I think someone wanted Mary Brady dead and saw to it that the women passengers of a stagecoach were gunned down, a riverboat was blown out of the water, and a train was derailed to make certain the job was done," Cody replied. "That doesn't add up to Bill and Melvin Quitman. I believe the wrong men are locked up back in the cells."

Patterson shook his head. "And I believe that these here telegrams of yours aren't worth the paper they're written on. I don't know why you're thinkin' the way you are, but it sounds like you've gone crazy in the head. I don't know a damned thing about riverboats bein' sunk or stagecoach robberies. What I *do* know is that I've got two men who had the reason for wreckin' a Texas and Pacific train—and I've arrested and charged them with that crime. Now the matter's out of my hands. What's to become of 'em is up to a judge and a jury. I ain't turnin' 'em loose because of a bunch of telegrams you got."

Cody picked up the telegrams and slipped them back in his vest pocket. He had hoped for better from Patterson but was prepared for this reaction. "I guess there's no need for me to remain here any longer, then. I'll be heading west on tomorrow morning's train."

"West?" The sheriff's eyes narrowed. "I thought you had work back in San Antonio."

"It'll hold," Cody replied, "until I've talked with Senator Calvin Brady."

He didn't wait to see Patterson's reaction, just turned and walked outside. A talk with Charity Quitman before he left Terrell was in order.

CHAPTER
▌▌▌▌▌▌▌▌▌▌▌▌▌▌▌▌▌▌ **14** ▌▌▌▌▌▌▌▌▌▌▌▌▌▌▌▌▌▌

Cody approached the Quitman farm at a slow, easy pace. He had no desire for Charity to misinterpret his intentions and suddenly pull out a rifle or shotgun and take his head off. The young woman was clearly capable of using a gun and would have no qualms about pulling the trigger on a man, if it served her purpose.

But Charity didn't appear on the porch with a shouldered weapon as Cody expected. Riding up to the house, he dismounted and tied his buckskin's reins to a cedar hitching post, then crossed the porch to the front door and rapped sharply.

He could hear muffled stirring, then the sound of footfalls. The door opened wide, and Charity stared at the Ranger, surprise, doubt, then anger washing over her face in the blink of an eye.

"You? What are you doing here?" she demanded.

Cody took off his hat. "I need to talk to you."

"You made it plain enough three days ago that we didn't have anything else to say to one another," she replied, her tone filled with bitterness. "I don't see that anything has changed since then."

"It has. First of all, I'm not a railroad detective. I'm a Texas Ranger. Second, I no longer believe your father and brother had anything to do with the Texas and Pacific wreck."

"Ranger?" She eyed him as though she wasn't certain she had heard him correctly—then her gaze focused on the badge pinned to his leather vest. "What are you trying to say, Colton?"

"Cody, actually. The name's Cody. And what I'm saying is that I think I've made a mistake. I don't have any proof—yet—but like I said, I believe your father and brother are innocent."

He dug into his vest pocket for the telegrams. "These are what changed my mind. Read them."

Charity took the yellow flimsies from his hand. She finished the first two, looked up, then motioned him into a small, neatly kept parlor. She sank onto a sofa while he stood watching her read the third wire. When she had finished, she looked up at him, confusion written on her face.

"I don't understand. Why would Senator Brady's wife make reservations on a train, a riverboat, and a stagecoach all on the same day?"

"That's exactly what I want to ask the senator," Cody said. "And why would those selfsame riverboat, train, and stagecoach all meet with disaster on exactly the same day?"

Charity glanced back at the telegrams and shook her head. "It doesn't make sense."

"Not unless someone was out to make certain Mary Brady never reached her destination," he said.

"But who?" Charity looked at him again. "Who would kill so many to make certain one woman died?"

"Someone hoping to hide one murder among many."

He frowned. The words had sprung from his mouth without thought; an instant later he recognized their significance. Whoever had killed Mary Brady had planned on concealing her murder among the bloody numbers of those killed on the train, the riverboat, and the stage. That same person also assumed that no one would ever make the connection between three crimes that had occurred so far apart in this vast state.

Had Cody not been aboard the *Big Cypress Runner* and had he not assisted in identifying the dead and survivors of that riverboat, he'd never have recognized Mary Brady's name. His was the luck of being in the wrong place at the right time.

Cody made a mental note to send another wire to Sheriff Howell in Jefferson, suggesting that the *Big Cypress Runner*'s boiler hadn't exploded on its own. He'd also send another telegram to headquarters and see if they could find out whom Mrs. Brady had intended to meet in St. Louis. It might be the person who had killed her and so many others.

"Do you think Calvin Brady is involved?" Charity asked.

Cody slowly shook his head. "There's nothing that points to him—but I have a feeling he knows why his wife made such elaborate plans to get out of the state." He paused and stared at the young woman, then added, "I know I've gotten your hopes up, but you have to realize that whatever happened to Mrs. Brady won't be easy to uncover. If she was involved in something that went against the law, her husband won't want to talk about it. He has a political career to protect, and that means keeping it free of scandal—especially if it involves his wife."

"But you don't think Pa and Melvin derailed the train?" she asked, wanting to reaffirm his early claim.

"No. I'm certain of that."

"That's a start." She stood, hope returned to her face.

"That might be all it ever is," he replied. "I want you to understand that up front. Nothing might ever come of this."

She gave a quick tilt of her head, a gesture that said she understood and approved. "But you'll be looking into it. That's more than I had when I woke up this morning."

"Your father and brother have gotten one break, at any rate," Cody told her. "The judge who was to hear their case died. Sheriff Patterson says it'll take at least a month to appoint another judge."

"Will Howard let them free during that time?" she asked. "He's seen these wires, hasn't he?"

Cody shook his head. "He's seen them, but he finds no significance in them. They'll have to stay in jail until I come up with proof that someone else wrecked the train."

Charity nibbled at her lower lip and sighed. "I suppose having them in jail awaiting trial is better than them sitting there waiting for the hangman. You'll find the person who did this in a month. I know you will."

"I can't promise you that." His gaze met hers and held it. "I can't promise anything, except I'll follow this to wherever it leads."

She smiled. "I can't ask for more than that."

Suddenly she threw her arms around his neck and planted a loud kiss of gratitude on his cheek. Cody recognized her innocent action for what it was—but his arms automatically encircled her waist. He drew her close, her slender, shapely body fitting so warmly against his, and his mouth covered her lips in a kiss fired by passion, not innocence.

To his surprise she didn't pull away from him. Instead, her arms tightened around his neck, and she melted against him. It was only when their lips parted that she apparently recognized what she had done. She eased from his arms and stepped back, her head hanging down, embarrassed by the display of desire—hers and his.

Cody felt a hollowness in his chest. Their intimacy had fled as quickly as it had come. He told himself it was best this way. He had no time for romantic entanglements. It wouldn't help find who had murdered Mary Brady.

"I'll be heading west on the morning train," he said, keeping his voice steady to hide his disappointment. "I don't know when I'll be back, but I'll contact you when I return."

"Please do that." Her eyes shyly avoided his. "And thank you."

"Thank me if and when I find something that will help your father and brother." Pulling on his Stetson, he turned and left the farmhouse, closing the door behind him. He tried not to look back when he mounted the gelding but couldn't help himself. Charity stood at the door's window, watching him.

Damn! He reprimanded himself for the kiss. He hadn't wanted to get personally involved in this case. But he was involved—and the name of that involvement was Charity Quitman.

Reining his horse around, he spurred the animal and left the farm at a fast canter.

Thoughts of Charity still befuddled his mind when he halted the buckskin beside a trickling creek halfway back to town. He dismounted and let the horse drink, then knelt and cupped his own hands into the water just upstream from the horse.

The rustle of grass and the creak of saddle leather snapped Cody's head up. Deputy Jeff Shiner guided his bay from behind a copse of black willows. The Ranger smiled at the deputy, who smiled back—as he lifted a cocked .44-caliber Colt and aimed it Cody's chest.

"You're a persistent man, Cody," the deputy said.

"Did Patterson send you out here to scare me off Mary Brady so he can keep that tin star of his nice and shiny?" Cody did his best not to sound intimidated by the threatening pistol. Trouble was, it was damned difficult not to be intimidated when looking down the barrel of a cocked revolver.

Jeff chuckled dryly. "Hell, Howard thinks I'm out tryin' to track down some missin' steers. He don't know nothin' 'bout me and Mrs. Brady."

Cody frowned, uncertain what this was about.

"No, I thought it was time you and me faced this head on and was through with it," Jeff continued. "I thought we was done that day I took a couple of potshots at you by them logs. You went runnin' off for Howard like I knew you would. Then he took you after Bill and Melvin."

A shiver crept down Cody's spine as the truth penetrated his mind. "Just like you wanted him to."

"That's right." Jeff's smile widened, but there was no humor in it. "Somethin' told me you wouldn't give up till you found yourself a train wrecker—so I gave you two of 'em. And just when I thought things was goin' smooth again, you showed up with them damned telegrams of yours." He shook his head. "It would've been a whole lot better for you if you hadn't."

"*You* pulled the spikes on those rails." The revelation left Cody stunned. He had never suspected the crippled young deputy.

"Right you are. And I was there when Mrs. Brady came stumblin' out of one of them overturned cars. Had to break her neck with my own hands. It was easy. She thought I was there to help. She came right to me. Didn't take more'n a second or two; then I mounted up and rode off. Nobody noticed I was there, 'specially after I covered my tracks.''

"You didn't do this on your own. Who were you working for?" Cody stalled for time while he tried to think. Jeff hadn't ridden out here for friendly conversation. He meant to use that Colt.

"It don't matter who. Leastwise, not to you. Not now. Let's just say I was doin' a favor for an old friend—for five thousand greenbacks," Jeff said. "It was all goin' slick as glass till you came up with them telegrams. You got too nosy, Cody. I wouldn't want no one goin' and findin' out it was me who killed Mrs. Brady. And there's only one way to make sure of that. . . ."

Cody saw the deputy tense as he prepared to pull the Colt's trigger. The Ranger didn't wait for the results. He leapt to the left, throwing himself to the ground.

The Colt barked, its report sounding like the roar of thunder. A soft thud whispered to Cody's right as the bullet slammed into the ground.

Cody's right hand found the holstered pistol on his hip. He wrenched it free, cocked the hammer, and aimed.

"Damn your eyes!" Jeff growled as he steadied his horse and readied his own Colt for another shot. "You ain't gettin' away from me! Not this day!"

But before the deputy could fire, Cody squeezed the trigger. The slug struck Jeff's chest dead center. The impact threw him back, arms jerking over his head as he tumbled from the saddle to the ground.

Cody cocked his pistol again and slowly rose, keeping the muzzle trained on the deputy. Jeff twitched and jerked as life fled his body, but he didn't rise. The body went still.

It took several moments before Cody's brain recognized that the fight was over. Two shots had been fired, and he was still alive. Holstering his revolver, he lifted the deputy's body from the ground and threw it belly down over the bay. Then he gathered the buckskin, mounted, and rode for Terrell, leading the dead killer's horse.

Howard Patterson barely contained himself as he listened—suspiciously—to Cody recount the gunfight. The Ranger could tell that the sheriff wanted to slap him into one of the jail cells and charge him with the murder of Jeff Shiner, especially when he repeated Jeff's admission of killing Mrs. Brady for five thousand dollars.

Cody had no doubt that he'd have been in the cell adjoining the Quitmans if a search of Jeff's one-room cabin at the eastern edge of town hadn't produced a rumpled brown envelope stuffed with hundred-dollar bills.

Patterson said nothing all the way back to his office. Only when he sank into the chair behind his desk and stared at the bundle of money before him did he say, "It don't make no sense. I gave him a good, honorable job."

"Guess he wanted more. What five thousand dollars can buy a man," Cody said. "And I want the man who paid him that money."

Patterson looked up. "You sure there wasn't somethin' between Jeff and Mary Brady? After all, he used to break broncs in her part of Texas."

Cody shook his head. "I think he knew her well enough to recognize her, but that's all. If there was anything between them, he'd have called her by her given name. Yet he kept saying 'Mrs. Brady.' No, he killed her for one thing—that money."

"Are you still headin' west in the mornin'?" Patterson asked.

Cody nodded.

"You'll be havin' company. I suddenly got me the urge to talk with Senator Calvin Brady."

CHAPTER
15

A quarter hour after he and Cody had stepped off the train in Fort Worth, Howard Patterson located the local sheriff's office. An hour after that he had secured two horses and tack, compliments of his fellow lawman, and he and the Ranger headed northwest for the town of Cross Bee—named not for an angry insect, but for the cattle brand of rancher and state senator Calvin Brady.

It was a two-day ride from Fort Worth before they sighted the town, which had been settled on the rolling plains that ran north from Fort Worth across the Red River and into Indian Territory. As in Fort Worth, Patterson paid an official visit to the local sheriff the moment they entered town. DeWitt Edwards and his deputy, James Cliff, welcomed them with a minimum of questions, then pointed them toward the local hotel—ten rooms built above a saloon called the Four Aces. After a brief respite for a shave and a hot bath to wash the trail dust from their bodies, Cody met with Patterson in his room.

"Did you see Edwards's face when we said we came to talk with Brady?" Patterson asked.

Cody had. It worried him. In all likelihood Brady already knew of their arrival and why they had come to Cross Bee. The Ranger had hoped to catch the senator off guard when he questioned him; now he'd have to use a straightforward tactic. Since that was the case, Cody was glad he hadn't hidden his identity. Brady now knew exactly who was on his trail.

Patterson rubbed a hand over his neck. "It ain't gonna do for the both of us to ride out to the Brady ranch. It'll look too strong arm, what with both of us wearin' a badge and all. I think you should talk with him alone to start things off. If there's need, we'll both meet with him tomorrow."

Silently relieved, Cody nodded. He had wanted to face Brady on his own but had been afraid his colleague would insist on questioning the senator. "You might talk with Edwards and his deputy and see what you can learn about Mary Brady," he suggested to Patterson.

"That's the way I figured it," the sheriff agreed. "If you're right about Mrs. Brady being involved in somethin' illegal, somebody in town would've caught wind of it. I'll start askin' around. Meet you back here 'round sundown?"

"Sundown," Cody confirmed.

Hurrying down the stairs and out of the saloon, he strode to the livery stable. He quickly saddled and mounted the dapple gray he had picked up in Fort Worth, then headed toward Brady's Cross B Ranch.

Cody reached the ranch, or at least the southern border of it, a mile out of town. Two hours and ten miles later he topped a grassy rise and looked down on the main ranch house. The structure was low slung, made from native rock mortared together, and roofed with cedar shakes. Behind the house stood a wooden windmill that pumped water into a rock tank. Behind the windmill were two barns, each ringed with corrals and pens. Except for ten horses in one of the corrals they were empty. Beyond the barns was another large rock structure. Cody squinted at it for several seconds before he recognized the immense building as a bunkhouse.

A creek ran through a deeply eroded gully a quarter of a mile west of the Cross B's headquarters, the same creek Cody had roughly followed to reach the compound. The trees and bushes growing beside the creek had been cleared for a half mile close to the house—a past precaution against Comanche and Kiowa attack, Cody guessed. A man didn't survive on the Texas plains by providing convenient cover for marauding braves.

That both those Indian nations had been defeated and were no longer an ever-present threat to these lands was evident in the saplings and bushes beginning to resettle on the creek bank. A man who feared Indian attack would never have let the chaparral push to its current scrubby height.

Clucking the gray forward, Cody reined the animal down the hill. Here and there cowhands moved about the ranch house and barns. If they noticed his approach—and there was no reason they wouldn't, since he rode in the open—they gave no indication of it. A strange rider should have drawn long stares. That he didn't said that the rancher had been alerted to his arrival and his men given instructions to pay little heed to any visitor. An uneasy feeling settled over the Ranger, and his right hand crept to his hip, the fingers touching the walnut grip of his holstered Colt.

The door to the ranch house opened when he halted the gray before one of three hitching rails in front of the structure. A tall, lanky young man no more than twenty-five years old stepped onto the wooden porch. He summed up Cody for a few seconds before he said, "Howdy. Name's Pete Brady. Can I help you?"

Cody introduced himself, making certain that the badge pinned to his vest was clearly visible. "I'd like to talk with Senator Calvin Brady, if I could trouble him for a few moments."

Another young man—a couple of years younger and an inch shorter than Pete—stepped outside. He, too, stared at Cody for several moments, sizing him up.

"George, this here's Mr. Cody, a Texas Ranger. He wants to talk with Pa."

Cody suppressed his surprise. The Brady name had been a giveaway that the two young men were related to the senator, but that they were his sons took him off guard. No one, not even the information from headquarters, had mentioned Brady had children—though no one would call either Pete or George a child.

George nodded. "My pa's in his study," he said, addressing Cody. "I'll take you back."

Cody followed the younger Brady son inside and down a narrow paneled hall that ran the length of the house. At least a dozen spacious rooms opened onto the hallway, and, glancing in as he passed them, Cody thought them furnished in an opulent fashion one wouldn't expect to find so far from Texas's urban centers. He could well imagine the small fortune it had taken to transport the furniture to the Cross B.

George stopped before a closed door and knocked on it. A resonating bass voice from within answered, "Come on in."

The opened door revealed a room of polished mahogany heavy with the sweet smell of peach oil. The walls were lined with bookcases filled with matching volumes bound in red leather, all perfectly arranged on the shelves. It seemed to Cody that the extensive library was little used—if used at all.

Across the room, beside three opened windows, stood an uncluttered desk, and seated in an overstuffed leather chair behind it was Senator Calvin Brady. He rose, smiled, and stuck out a paw of a hand when George introduced the Ranger. Brady then dismissed his son and waved Cody to another chair placed in front of his desk.

Father and sons had been cut from the same cloth. All three had rugged faces with features that appeared to have been chiseled by the elements. Like Pete and George, Calvin Brady was long and lean. Cody doubted there was one extra ounce of fat on the body beneath the black suit Brady wore. The senator was one of those men whose age might be forty or seventy, if his weathered face alone was used as a gauge. But Cody didn't have to guess; the background sketch had given the politician's age as forty-five. Streaks of silver ran through a full head of dark-brown hair, though there was no hint of gray in the neat mustache that covered his upper lip.

"I've been expecting a visit from you ever since I heard the state had assigned a Ranger to investigate the Texas and Pacific train wreck outside of Terrell," the senator said. He leaned back in his chair and tented his fingers. "I suspect your being here has something to do with my wife being on that train."

The Ranger couldn't hide the surprise that danced over his

face. So Brady had known about the investigation before Cody had ever arrived in town. The senator's spy network was damn good. And he didn't bandy words, either. Cody began to wonder about the wisdom of coming here in the open. The man obviously had had time to prepare for this meeting. Working undercover might have allowed the Ranger more leeway.

"Yes, sir," Cody answered. "I do have a few questions about your wife." He glanced at the door to the study. "I'm certain your sons were hard hit by their mother's death."

"Mary wasn't their mother. She was my third wife," Brady said. "Married my sons' mother, Susan, when I was fifteen. Took a second wife after Susan died when I was twenty-five. Elsie passed on after eight years. Mary and I said our vows five years ago. This country seems to be harder on women than it is on men."

Brady's tone was cool and matter-of-fact, almost detached. He spoke of three women he had spent his life with, but he might just as well have been describing hunting dogs he had owned over the years. He was far from the grieving widower Cody had expected to find.

"But it isn't my first two wives you're interested in," Brady said. "You want to know about Mary."

"Just about her travel arrangements," Cody replied, explaining his discovery that Mary Brady had made three diverse reservations for her trip to St. Louis. He didn't mention the disasters that had struck each of the three. Something about Brady's manner said he already knew of them. "Why would your wife make such elaborate plans?"

Brady gave a diffident shrug, an action that struck Cody as odd. "I know nothing about a riverboat or a stage. All I know is that Mary intended to travel east by train, then by coach to the Mississippi. From there she was to take a riverboat upriver to St. Louis, where she planned to spend a month visiting with her sister. Mary was originally from Missouri."

For the next hour Brady answered Cody's questions and interspersed his own about the investigation into the wreck. Several times Cody brought up the travel arrangements Mary Brady had made, but the senator avowed knowledge of the train only. And he didn't so much as blink when Cody suggested as delicately as he could that Mary Brady might have been fleeing Texas or someone within the state.

"I assure you that Mary had no reason to travel north except the desire to visit with her only sister," Brady said in the same distant tone he had used throughout the interview. "I have no idea why my wife made more than one travel plan, but I can say without a doubt that whatever her intentions were, they were completely innocent."

Brady paused and glanced out a window. "Now, Mr. Cody, if you have no further questions, I have other business to attend to."

Cody had no choice but to go along with the dismissal. Rising, he thanked the senator for his time, adding, "I'll be staying in town a few days. If anything else occurs to me, mind if I talk with you again?"

"Surely," Brady said. "Ride out whenever you like. You might have to wait a while, though. I like to keep an eye on my men and how they're handling the stock. But feel free to call."

"It don't sound like you learned a hell of a lot more'n I did," Howard Patterson said as he sawed into a steak that covered the majority of his dinner plate.

Cody shook his head as he cut a bite from his own steak. "Brady's a cool one, all right—maybe even cold. Every word he said to me was like an actor giving a performance. Like he had prepared his answers days ago." He cautiously glanced around the saloon, but the five other patrons had no apparent interest in the two visitors or their conversation. "I'm damn certain that Brady knew exactly what I was going to ask him before I even asked it."

The lawman swallowed the steak he chewed, then said, "If he is coverin' up somethin' his wife was into, that'd make sense."

"I suppose," Cody agreed. "But Brady acted like a man who wasn't trying to protect his dead wife's reputation so much as he was stepping around dirt that might splatter on his own cuffs.''

The sheriff snorted. ''Politicians are like that. But I reckon he's tryin' to keep his wife's affairs private. Seems that Senator Brady and his third wife weren't exactly lyin' in a bed of roses.''

Cody hiked an eyebrow. ''How's that?''

''Sheriff Edwards and Deputy Cliff were pretty tight-lipped about Brady, but they said there were rumors earlier this year that Mrs. Brady had taken to findin' comfort outside the marriage bed,'' Patterson replied. ''Reckon you know she was twenty-five when she married Brady, and he was forty. She was quite the belle of the ball down in Austin. Young bucks swarmin' all around her. Lots of folks were left with their jaws adanglin' when she up and married Brady.''

Cody's eyes narrowed. ''Are you saying she had a lover?'' he asked, astonished.

''Maybe more'n one.'' Patterson took another bite of steak and chewed it for several seconds. ''Edwards won't say much 'cept that he had seen Mrs. Brady's eye rovin' on more'n one occasion. Seems it might have been more'n just age separatin' Calvin and Mary Brady. Edwards hinted that maybe Brady wasn't man enough anymore to keep a woman happy.''

''Did he give you any names of the men Mary Brady supposedly had affairs with?'' Cody's mind raced. Marital difficulties! He hadn't considered that.

''Just one,'' Patterson answered. ''A cowboy out of El Paso called Drew Randolph. He was one of Brady's top hands—in line for foreman. Then back in January Brady up and fired him. Edwards heard several Cross B hands mention that Brady threatened to kill Randolph if he ever saw him in Texas again. The last Edwards saw of this Randolph, he was ridin' hard and scared for the Red River.''

Cody put down his knife and stared at his fellow lawman. ''Maybe he rode all the way to St. Louis.'' Piece by piece a dark picture was falling into place. Had Drew Randolph sent word for Mary Brady to meet him? If so, then was it her husband she had fled here in Texas?

He pushed from the table and stood up. "I need to send a wire to headquarters. Have them check something out for us."

"Hold on a minute," Patterson said, waving him back to his chair. "There's somethin' else."

Cody sat back down.

"It's about Jeff Shiner," the sheriff said. "Seems that Jeff was workin' for Brady out on the Cross B when he busted up his leg."

Cody leaned closer to his companion. "Are you certain?"

"Certain," Patterson said with a nod. "And if you're thinkin' what I'm thinkin', then we both got a good idea where Jeff got that five thousand dollars we found in his room."

"A damned good idea," Cody said, once more standing. "Now all we have to do is prove it."

CHAPTER
16

Cross Bee was a town of ten shops and stores. Together and on their own, Cody and Howard Patterson had talked with each of the proprietors of those establishments and anyone else who would pause long enough to listen to their questions. What they had learned was nothing.

Except that folks in Cross Bee were frightened when it came to speaking about Senator Calvin Brady.

They averted their eyes, and their hands trembled whenever the possibility that Mary Brady had been having an affair with one of her husband's cowhands was mentioned. And the idea was quickly—too quickly—scoffed at.

Even Sheriff DeWitt Edwards, who had first mentioned Mary Brady's infidelity to Howard Patterson, now seemed to have forgotten ever knowing a cowboy from El Paso named Drew Randolph. He lightheartedly laughed off the notion that Calvin Brady's wife had been cheating on her husband.

"You know how it is in small towns," Edwards retorted. "Men are just as bad as the women. Got to have something to talk about. If things seem too dull, then they just sort of make things up to keep it interesting," he said. "Hell, they're all like a bunch of old hens. Ninety-nine out of a hundred things a man hears here is nothing but rumor."

As Cody walked down the street, he could almost smell the fear in the air that his presence stirred up. Cross Bee had been born and continued to survive by servicing the Brady ranch. The other ranches in the area were small, family operations;

Calvin Brady ran an empire. The real money in Cross Bee came out of the pockets of Brady and the men he employed on his spread. Without the Brady ranch, the town would dry up and blow away in a matter of days. Its citizenry wasn't likely to speak out against the man responsible for keeping food on their tables.

Cody glanced westward. The sun would soon be hidden behind one of the rises the locals called mountains—and he'd have spent one more day in Cross Bee without having moved an inch closer to learning who had paid Jeff Shiner five thousand dollars to kill Mary Brady.

Frustrated, he cursed the citizens of the town for their cowardice. But he had to admit that if he stood in their shoes, he'd react the same way. Speaking out about Calvin and Mary Brady in this town would be tantamount to suicide.

Continuing down the street, Cody walked toward the small, whitewashed telegraph office as he had done every morning, noon, and evening for two days. Until he received word from headquarters on Mary Brady's plans in St. Louis, he had run out of moves.

And even when the answers arrived, he had no guarantee they'd be the ones he hoped for. Calvin Brady may have told the truth when he said his wife had gone to visit her sister. Cody had no evidence to disprove the senator's contention— only a gut feeling that the money given to Jeff Shiner had come from him.

The Ranger thought about the father and son who sat in a jail cell in Terrell, awaiting a murder trial. The Quitmans were certain to keep an appointment with a hangman unless—

He shoved the gloomy notion aside. He couldn't dwell on what might happen; he needed to focus his thoughts on the here and now. Had he overlooked something? Maybe not talked with the one person in town unafraid to speak the truth about the Brady marriage?

He scowled darkly as he entered the telegraph office. The click-a-click of a telegraph key drew his attention to the operator, who held up a hand to silence him before he spoke and continued jotting down the letters that came across the wire in bursts of dots and dashes. Abruptly the telegraph key went silent. The telegrapher tapped out a signal to confirm that the message had been received.

"I think this is what you've been waiting for, Mr. Cody," the telegrapher said as he picked up a pad of yellow paper and began to transcribe the message. "Give me a moment to get this all written out in a readable fashion."

Impatiently, Cody watched the man carefully write out the message. It seemed to take hours for him to form each of the long, flowing letters, as though he were completing a school penmanship lesson rather than transcribing a telegraph wire.

"There!" The telegrapher tore the sheet of paper from the pad.

Cody scanned the message and his heart began racing. Patterson had to see this! He flipped the telegrapher a two-bit piece as a tip, left the office, and hurried down the street.

Reaching the saloon, he made his way to the stairs and took them two at a time, then knocked on the sheriff's door. Not waiting for an answer, he opened the door and stepped into the room.

He froze as he straddled the threshold. Charity Quitman sat by the window in the room's only chair.

Patterson, who was perched on the side of his bed, looked up at Cody. "Guess who I found snooping around in your room when I came up from supper."

"I wasn't snooping," Charity protested indignantly. "I told you, I was looking for Mr. Cody."

"What are you doing here?" Cody asked, staring at the young woman and not wanting to believe his eyes.

"I had to make sure you two were handling this correctly," she answered. "After all, it's my father's and brother's lives you're dealing with. That's too important a matter to leave in the hands of strangers."

"Dammit, girl, I'm hardly a stranger," Patterson said. "And you've no business being here."

After the kiss he and Charity had shared, Cody didn't feel like they were strangers, either, but he said, "Howard's right. This is no place for you—especially now."

"I'm here, and that's all there is to that," she said with finality in her voice. "Why don't one of you ask me if I'm hungry, then take me downstairs and buy me supper? I haven't eaten since breakfast . . . and that was only two cold biscuits."

Ignoring Charity's remark, Patterson asked the Ranger, "What's so special about now?"

"I got the wire I've been waiting for." Cody held up the telegram. "It just came in."

"What wire?" Charity asked.

Patterson ignored her again. "Does it say what I think it says?"

"And more." Cody settled on the side of the bed, passing the paper to the sheriff. "First off, Brady was telling only half the truth. His wife *was* intending to visit her sister in St. Louis—but the senator failed to mention that from St. Louis Mary Brady had made riverboat reservations to take her up the Missouri to the Dakota Territory."

"All the way to Fargo," Patterson said, reading aloud.

"Right. All the way to Fargo. And do you know what that means?"

It was Charity who answered, "Divorce! Mary Brady intended to divorce her husband!"

"You win the cigar," Cody said, nodding.

It didn't surprise him that Charity had so quickly made the connection. Dakota divorces were infamous across the United States, and Fargo was considered the divorce capital of the territory. All one had to do was file for a divorce in Fargo, and within a matter of hours the binds of marriage were neatly—and legally—untied.

"Damn!" Patterson spat. "Divorce! The bastard killed twenty people on that train to stop her from divorcing him!"

"As well as those women on the stage and the men and women on the riverboat," Cody added. "It's a bloody tally just to stop one woman."

But he was certain that that was the truth of it. Calvin Brady was an ambitious man with his eye set on the governor's mansion in Austin. From all Cody could gather, only a major scandal would stop Brady from achieving that goal. Divorce would have been such a scandal. It probably would've cost him the office of state senator, too.

Realizing that her husband would stop at nothing to prevent her from leaving him, Mary Brady no doubt hoped that three separate plans for escape from Texas would do the trick. Trouble was, she hadn't counted on Brady finding a way of blocking all her avenues. All except one, and that way led to the grave.

Cody shivered, envisioning the horror of the riverboat explosion. So many people dead just to ensure that Mary Brady died, too. It was an unbelievably ruthless plan. And all Brady had needed to do was provide blood money to men like Jeff Shiner to see that it was completed. They had done the dirty work. Brady had never soiled his hands.

"This ain't hard evidence," Patterson noted, handing the telegram back to the Ranger.

"But it's a motive," Cody said. "That's a start, and that's more than we had a few minutes ago."

"Where do you go from here?" Charity asked, concern knitting her brow.

Cody wasn't certain. "Well, we can sit around hoping someone in Austin finds the men who robbed that stage and they point a finger at Brady. Or we can pray Sheriff Howell in Jefferson can prove someone deliberately blew the *Big Cypress Runner* out of the water, and he can find that one someone who'll sing like a bird. Or we can start with Jeff Shiner's five thousand dollars and try to trace it back to Brady."

He liked the last idea. It held more promise than putting their hopes on men who had yet to be apprehended and in all likelihood would never be. Five thousand dollars was a large sum of money, hard for a man to hide. If he could prove Brady had recently withdrawn the sum from a bank, it might be the thread needed to tie the senator to the deputy.

"Whatever we decide to do," Cody continued, "It's too late to do it tonight. I suggest we get a good night's sleep and explore all our possibilities tomorrow morning."

"Agreed," Patterson said with an approving nod. "One of

us ought to go downstairs and see about gettin' Charity here a room for the night."

"I'll do it," Cody said without hesitation. "I'll also see that she has the supper she mentioned earlier." He glanced at the young woman and received a smile.

"Then why don't you do just that and let me get on to bed?" Patterson grumbled.

Cody and Charity didn't argue. They stepped into the hall, closing the door behind them.

The young woman turned to the Ranger. "Howard was right, wasn't he? You're still a long way from proving that Brady had anything to do with the death of his wife, aren't you?"

"A longer way than you want to know," Cody admitted. "If something is going to happen, I'm going to have to make it happen. And I'm not sure exactly how to go about that. Brady's not stupid. He planned out his wife's murder with great care. He's only made one mistake so far: He thought the riverboat sinking, the train wreck, and the stagecoach robbery would never be connected. My hope is that if he's made one mistake, he's made others. If he has, I'll find them."

Cody made that promise to a woman who had died saving a little boy as much as he did to Charity.

"I know you will." Charity rose on her tiptoes and pressed her mouth to his.

His arms encircled her slender waist, and this time there was no shy withdrawal. Her own arms slipped to his back, returning his embrace. When they parted, she stared up at him with a pleased smile on her lips and unspoken promises for a future time lighting her eyes.

"I think you said something about supper," she said softly. Taking his hand, she held it all the way downstairs.

CHAPTER
||||||||||||||||||||||||||||| **17** |||||||||||||||||||||||||||||

Cody!"

    An insistent voice called his name. He opened his eyes and tried to blink away the harsh sunlight that flooded through the hotel window. It wouldn't go away, so he closed his eyes again and attempted to sink back into sleep. Last night had provided little rest. He had tossed and turned for hours while his mind wrestled with how to deal with Calvin Brady.

In fact, the only good thing—things—Cody remembered about the night were the two kisses Charity had given him. The second had come as they said good night outside her room. The long, lingering kiss had brought a disappointed sigh from her throat when they had parted.

"Cody!"

The persistent voice called to him again. Something nudged his shoulder.

"No need to play possum, Cody. I got an invite for you from the senator," the voice said.

Groaning, Cody rolled over and stared up at Pete Brady, Calvin Brady's older son, who shook his head and said, "Most men in this country haven't got time to sleep late."

"What do you want?" Cody demanded.

"Me? I don't have any wants from you," Pete answered. "But the senator, that's another story. He wants you and Sheriff Patterson to come on out to the Cross B. My pa wants to talk to you two about a telegram you received late yesterday . . ."

Cody silently cursed. In his excitement last night he had forgotten about the telegrapher. The man had obviously seen to it that Calvin Brady had gotten a copy of the message from Kansas City.

"The senator said you two were to be at the main house at straight-up noon." Without waiting for Cody to respond, Pete turned and crossed the hotel room to the door. He opened it wide, then looked back at the Ranger. "Oh, yeah, there's more I'm supposed to tell you. In case you have any ideas about not showing up, a friend of yours is visiting out at the ranch—that pretty young filly you were seen kissing last night. A couple of the boys will be more than willing to have her, if you don't show up to take her home."

A wicked grin split Pete's face, and he winked lewdly to make certain Cody understood Charity's fate should the Ranger not accept Brady's invitation. Then he turned and left the room, slamming the door after him.

Cody threw back the sheet and leapt from the bed. Within three minutes he was fully dressed and rushing into Patterson's room. "He's taken Charity! The bastard's got Charity!"

Sleepy-eyed, the lawman blinked up at him from the bed. "Who's got what?"

"Charity! Brady's got Charity out at the Cross B." While he dragged the sheriff from his bed, Cody explained Pete's unexpected visit and the reason behind it. "We've got until noon to get out there."

"If he knows about that telegram, then he knows we're on to him," Patterson said as he pulled on his breeches and shirt, then tugged on his boots. "And I don't reckon he'd like us to get away with what we suspect."

"That's the way I see it. Brady must have at least fifty hands on the Cross B. Fifty against two. Those aren't my kind of odds."

"I'd make it more like a hundred cowboys ridin' for him," Patterson said as he strapped on his gun belt. "Fifty or a hundred, it makes little difference. All it takes is one bullet to bring a man down."

Cody opened his pocket watch. Eight o'clock. Four hours

until they had to be at the ranch. "It's time we let Sheriff Edwards in on what's happening," he said.

Patterson nodded. "We can use all the help we can get. And you might fire off a wire to Major Jones, just to make sure someone knows what happened to us in case we never come back from the Cross B."

The idea of a last-minute telegram wired to San Antonio didn't sit well with Cody. It smacked of a finality he wasn't prepared to face. But the sheriff was right. If Brady kept tabs on the telegrams that came and went in this town, such a wire just might be the insurance they needed to make certain the morning outside wasn't the last one they saw.

"We'll talk with the sheriff first," Cody said, "then send the wire."

"Lead the way," Patterson said. "We aren't any closer to gettin' Charity back standin' 'round here, flappin' our jaws."

Neither Edwards nor James Cliff, his deputy, was in the office, and it didn't appear that they expected to be there anytime that day. A quickly scrawled message on the back of a wanted poster tacked to Edwards's desk stated that the sheriff and the deputy had learned of a band of rustlers working the northern portion of the county and had ridden out to track them down.

Patterson snorted. "Convenient, huh?" He ripped the note from the desk and crumpled it into a ball that he threw into a corner.

"Very convenient," Cody agreed. "Pete probably stopped by to see Edwards before he dropped in on me and suggested that Senator Brady would be pleased if Edwards and Cliff made themselves scarce today."

Patterson didn't disagree with that scenario. Instead, he walked over to a rifle rack and pulled down two Sharps repeaters. He tossed one to Cody, then rummaged among the boxes of shells on the bottom shelf of the rack, finding cartridges for the rifles.

"No scattergun today?" Cody asked, surprised that the lawman passed over a shotgun.

Patterson shook his head. "If we let Brady's men get close

enough to use a shotgun, we'll both be dead.'' He handed half the shells to Cody, then began loading his rifle.

Cody followed suit, then put the remaining sheils in a pocket. ''We still have a telegram to send. It might be our only protection.''

''Then let's get that damned thing sent. Brady's moving too fast to suit me. It's time we kicked a few spokes out of his wheels,'' the sheriff said, motioning the Ranger from the office.

Apparently Sheriff Edwards wasn't the only one in Cross Bee who had been warned to stay clear of Cody and Patterson. As the pair stepped outside, passersby ducked into shops and stores, leaving the street completely deserted.

''I've never seen no ghost town''—Patterson's gaze darted over the town while he kept the rifle ready—''but I suspect it feels a lot like this.''

Cody had read about abandoned mining towns out west and decided that this was probably worse. As he strode toward the telegraph office, he could feel dozens of pairs of eyes on him. If a corpse could walk, he was certain it would feel like he did at that moment.

The telegrapher glanced up as the men walked into his cramped office. A forced smile spread across his face. ''Gentlemen, how can I help you this morning?''

''I need to send a wire to San Antonio,'' Cody answered.

The telegrapher handed him a pad and pencil. ''Write your message down, and I'll get it off just as soon as the wire's up again.''

''*What?*'' Patterson yelped. His eyes narrowed suspiciously, and he took a threatening step toward the telegrapher.

''The wire's down,'' the man explained with a nervous swallow. He reached out and tapped the key with a finger. ''See, it's dead. I'm certain the company's got men out, trying to find where it went down. They'll get it up as soon as they can. But I wouldn't go holding my breath until they do. Last time a storm brought it down, it took a week to repair.''

''Why, you little son of a—''

Cody grabbed Patterson's arm as it shot for the telegrapher's throat. "Let him be. It's not him; it's Brady. He's a step ahead of us. He had the wire cut."

"Damn!" Desperation flashed in the sheriff's eyes. "He's herdin' us right where he wants us."

Cody steered him out the door and toward the livery stable. "Look, I started this. There's no need for you to ride out to the ranch. I'll go alone. Matter of fact, it might be wise if you rode for Fort Worth and let others know what we've found out."

"It would be damned stupid," Patterson retorted. "If Brady's smart enough to cut the telegraph wire, he's smart enough to have men waitin' outside of town to bushwhack us if we try to ride for help. No, we'll ride out to the ranch together."

"Have it your way," Cody said with a shrug, grateful to have the sheriff at his side.

"It ain't my way," Patterson replied as they entered the stable. "It's just the way it is."

Saddling their horses, they mounted, double-checked the loads in their rifles and pistols, then moved out. Cody opened his pocket watch again; it read nine o'clock—three hours until they were due at the Cross B's main house.

Keeping their horses at a brisk walk, they rode in silence. There was nothing left to say. They were two men going up against everyone who rode for Calvin Brady. Odds were they wouldn't return.

Using the tree-lined creek to guide them, they rode in a northeasterly direction, their eyes constantly sweeping the rolling hills. The only movement Cody saw were steers grazing in the distance and a red-tailed hawk soaring high above.

Balancing the Sharps in the crook of his left arm, the Ranger used a shirtsleeve to wipe away the sweat beading his forehead. The sun was less than halfway to its zenith, and already the air felt like the heart of a blast furnace.

Doubt nibbled at Cody's mind. They were two crazy hombres riding into an obvious trap on a hope and a prayer that they could rescue a woman who in all likelihood was already dead. What could two expect to do against a hundred?

Even the defenders of the Alamo hadn't faced such lopsided odds—and history told what had occurred at the Alamo.

A distant rustle of grass jerked Cody's head to the right, and his gaze raced up a knoll. Five riders, each carrying a rifle, crested the hill from the other side. Spotting Cody and Patterson, the riders shouted angrily and charged down the long slope directly at the lawmen. Apparently Senator Brady had no intention of allowing his invited guests to reach the Cross B's ranch house.

Cody swung the Sharps to his shoulder. His finger closed around the rifle's trigger and squeezed down just as five barking reports sounded. Hot lead whined through the air around him as he fired the rifle. But the shot went wide, and all five men still rode down on them.

A groan came from behind Cody, and he twisted around. Patterson rocked from side to side in the saddle, his right hand clutching his left shoulder. Blood seeped between his fingers. Despite his wound, the sheriff had somehow held on to his rifle, but he had lost the reins, which now rode high on his horse's neck.

Gripping the Sharps and his own reins in his left hand, Cody swung the gray's head around. He reached out and grabbed the bridle of Patterson's mount near the bit. A glance over a shoulder revealed that the riders hadn't slowed.

"Hold on!" Cody ordered his colleague.

He spurred the gray forward while clucking to Patterson's bay. The two horses broke into a run, their long legs stretching to a full gallop as the pursuing riders opened up with another volley.

Cody forced himself to ignore the angry buzz of bullets that cut the air around him. He focused on the trees and brush lining the creek ahead. An open prairie was no place to make a stand with a wounded man.

The five riders fired another round just as Cody and Patterson reached the heavy underbrush. The shots were high and tore into the leaves overhead. Cody jerked back on the reins beside a twin-trunked willow, halting his gray and the sheriff's bay. He threw his right leg over the gray's neck and jumped to the ground, then raced around the bay to help Patterson from the saddle. There was no need. The sheriff had managed to slip out of the stirrups and slide from his mount's back.

"Get behind those trees!" Cody shouted, pivoting to face the riders.

He hiked the Sharps to his shoulder, took a bead on the nearest man, and fired. He didn't wait to see if his shot had been true. Leaping to the right, he threw himself to the ground and rolled behind another willow ten feet from Patterson.

The sharp crack of four rifles answered his round. Again the bullets tore through leaves as they went high and wide. But the shots spooked the horses. They snorted and bolted through the underbrush, and when they reached the edge of the steep gully, the animals leapt down, then ran through the shallow creek, heading toward town.

"Only four shots! That means you got one!" Patterson said, scooting around. Using only his right arm, he managed to shoulder his rifle, aim down the barrel, and fire. "Damn! Missed."

Though the shot was wild, it illustrated the danger facing Brady's men. The four riders split; two reined to the northeast, while the remaining two spurred southwest. Cody tried to get another bead, but the men disappeared into the line of trees on both sides of him.

"They're goin' to try to come at us two ways at once," Patterson said. He looked at his left shoulder and grimaced. "This ain't no time to be on foot."

Patterson was stating the obvious, Cody thought. He looked quickly from right to left. It'd only be a matter of time before the four riders came barreling down on them through the trees.

"How's your arm?" he asked in a voice not much above a whisper.

"It hurts worse than it looks." Patterson gritted his teeth as he cautiously flexed arm and shoulder. "Bullet grazed me. Took out a chunk of meat, and its bleedin', but it ain't as bad as it could be. I can still use the arm."

"You think you can make it to the other side of the creek?" Cody asked, gesturing over his shoulder.

Patterson stared at the creek for a long moment. When he looked back at his companion, he smiled conspiratorially, having deduced what Cody had in mind. "It just might work. And sittin' here ain't goin' to do either of us any good."

"Then let's give it a try."

Cocked rifles in hand, they moved back to the edge of the gully. While Cody covered him, Patterson slid down the bank of the arroyo, splashed across the creek, and scurried up the other side. The Ranger followed suit. As they hid themselves in the thick brush, Cody looked across to the spot they had vacated. There was no sign of the horsemen.

"Now we wait," he whispered, "and hope they didn't catch sight of us."

The wait was less than five minutes. Howling like Comanches, the riders spurred their mounts through the line of trees to converge on the two lawmen they had been sent to kill.

Only the lawmen weren't there. Cody smiled as he raised his Sharps. The ruse had worked.

He held his trigger finger, waiting until the pursuers were directly across from him. He could see the perplexed expression on their faces—and then they looked to the opposite bank. He squeezed the trigger.

Patterson's rifle thundered an instant after Cody's.

On the other side of the creek two men groaned and fell from their saddles. Startled by the unexpected reversal of their planned ambush, the remaining two horsemen jerked the heads of their mounts around and retreated through the dense thicket.

"They ain't givin' up," Patterson declared and shot a glance at Cody as the riders disappeared from sight. "They know damned well Calvin Brady won't accept nothin' for an excuse if they ride back without us belly down across a horse."

Cody swore. Horses concerned him, all right, but not being draped across the back of one. The mounts of the two men they had killed were gone, and he could only hope that they weren't now racing back to their barn. Riderless horses were certain to bring more of Brady's men—and the two out there were enough.

"Wha'd'ya say we slip on back to the other side," Patterson suggested. "No need to stay put in one spot and make it easy for them bushwhackers."

Cody agreed. He and the sheriff darted from the trees in a crouched run and slid into the gully.

But this time the riders were ready for the maneuver. Breaking from the trees, they reined their mounts down the steep embankment, then charged straight for Cody and Patterson, rifles blazing.

Cody dropped to a knee in the middle of the rocky creek while slugs bit into the water around him. He shouldered the Sharps and sighted down the barrel on the horseman directly in front of him, then pulled the trigger.

The shot slammed into the rider's chest, and his body crumpled inward, then flew backward under the impact. He dropped from the saddle, landing faceup in the stream.

To Cody's left Patterson fired. His shot also found its target, dropping the last rider beside his cohort.

There wasn't time for even a congratulatory nod between the two men. The riderless horses continued to charge down the stream. Throwing themselves to opposite banks, Cody and Patterson barely managed to escape the hooves that would have succeeded where bullets had failed.

Cody picked himself up as the horses passed, watching the animals disappear at a dead run down the creek. "They won't stop till they reach home."

Patterson's gaze was on the men they had killed. "That's five down and ninety-five to go." He glanced at Cody. "Any ideas on what to do next?"

"Yeah. Tear off that shirtsleeve and bandage your arm," Cody answered. "Then, I guess, we walk."

CHAPTER

‖‖‖‖‖‖‖‖‖‖‖‖‖‖‖‖‖‖ **18** ‖‖‖‖‖‖‖‖‖‖‖‖‖‖‖‖‖‖

Riders!'' Cody signaled Howard Patterson to find cover.
The sheriff immediately dropped to a crouch and scurried into a stand of wild persimmon bushes. Cody did the same, pressing low to the ground as ten mounted men crossed the creek, heading for Calvin Brady's ranch.

''Damn!'' the sheriff muttered, wiping the dust from his face. ''That was close.''

Almost too close, Cody thought. The riders had passed a mere ten feet from their position. Sheer luck had provided the dense persimmons to shelter them—and it was only a matter of time until their luck ran out. Since entering the gully and starting the long walk toward the Cross B's headquarters, Cody and Patterson had managed to dodge seven such patrols.

Patterson rolled to his back and heaved a labored breath. ''Brady's men are as thick as fleas on a hound in summer. He must have 'em crisscrossin' the whole prairie lookin' for us.''

Cody studied his companion. The sheriff was holding up better than he had expected, considering his shoulder wound and the relentless heat.

''If any of those loose horses made it back to the main house, Brady's got to figure we're out here,'' Cody said. ''He won't stop looking until he finds us.''

Patterson closed his eyes. ''Yeah. The same thought crossed my mind. Dark'll slow 'em up a mite, but come mornin' they'll be looking for us again. Sooner or later one of 'em's goin' to stumble atop us.''

"Then we'll just have to see to it that we aren't around in the morning."

Cody scooted toward the edge of the persimmon bushes and parted a couple of branches to check on the riders. What he saw surprised him. Before he could say anything, Patterson asked, "Tell me, Cody, if we reach the ranch house—and that's a big if in my mind—have you given any thought as to just how we're goin' to get Charity away from Brady?" In a softer voice, he added, "That is, if she's still alive."

Instead of replying, Cody waved the sheriff to his side. "Howard, take a look at this."

Complying, Patterson looked through the branches Cody held apart. The ranch house was dead ahead. The sheriff looked at the Ranger and grinned. "I'll be damned! We did it."

"That we did," Cody said, returning Patterson's grin. "I didn't realize we had come so far."

"It seemed about a hundred times farther to me," Patterson muttered, shifting to his back again and closing his eyes. "You still ain't answered my question. How the hell are we goin' to get into that house? It ain't like we can just walk up and go in through the front door."

"Maybe that's exactly what we should do."

Patterson's eyes snapped open, and he stared at the Ranger. "Have you gone and lost your mind?"

"Could be," Cody replied, shrugging. "But here's the way I see it. . . ."

The sun set at 8:36 P.M. by Cody's watch. Another thirty minutes passed before dusk deepened to twilight. In that shadowy time separating day from night, Cody and Patterson crawled from under the persimmon bushes and eased back into the gully. Using the wash's high banks to hide their presence, they darted along the creek until they reached the middle of that portion of bank that had once been cleared of vegetation. Then they crept halfway up the bank and peered over the edge.

Most of the activity around the ranch house centered on the

barns as Brady's men returned their horses to stalls and corrals for the night, then headed for the bunkhouse. But it was clear that the senator was prepared for unannounced visitors during the night. Two pairs of guards were patrolling around the main house; another two guards stood at one of the barns' doors.

"So much for goin' in the front door," Patterson said with a shake of his head. "There ain't no way we'll get within two hundred yards of that house. Those men ain't blind."

"They will be—or at least close to it," Cody said, speaking his thoughts aloud. "We're only a day shy of a full moon tonight, but there'll be a half hour of dark before the moon comes up. If we move in low and fast, we can make it."

He pointed to the two pairs of guards circling the ranch house. Each pair kept half the length of the house between them. "All we have to do is creep up as close to the side of the house as we can and wait to make our move."

Patterson studied the quarter of a mile between their position and the house. "Gettin' there will be nothin' short of a miracle."

"Then we'll make ourselves a miracle." The bravado in Cody's voice didn't match the doubt in his mind. A thousand things could go wrong before they reached the house. And if they succeeded in crossing the quarter mile, they'd have four guards to deal with.

"Brady's bound to have more men inside the house," Patterson pointed out.

"We'll handle them once we're in."

Cody watched the guards, getting a feel for their routine. Like clockwork they moved, taking a minute to make a full circuit of the house.

Finally, when the last glow of twilight faded from the sky, Cody and Patterson rolled over the top of the gully. They rose to their knees and examined the house one last time. Then they crept toward the structure in a crouch.

Cody moved as carefully as possible. A foot misplaced on an unseen rock might spill him to the ground and alert the men guarding the house, who were almost invisible in the darkness except when they were silhouetted against one of the brightly lit windows.

Fifty yards from the house Cody and Patterson halted. They watched the guards make their circuit of the low-slung structure three times. As the guards began their fourth circle, the lawmen darted forward. Fearing the sharp bark of a rifle announcing their discovery, they shot through the night. Only when they stood with their backs pressed against the side of the house did they feel they had succeeded—at least with the first step of their rescue plan.

The soft footfalls of the approaching pair of guards grew closer. Inching toward the corner of the house, Cody hefted his rifle high to use as a club. Patterson imitated his action. Then they waited.

The guards came around the corner together. Cody's rifle descended, as did Patterson's. Two spongy, muffled thuds sounded as the rifle barrels found their targets. Both guards dropped to the ground without muttering so much as a groan.

Dragging the two unconscious men out of sight, Cody and Patterson hiked their rifles again and returned to the corner of the house. A minute later the second pair of guards joined their cronies on the ground.

"The front door?" Patterson asked in a whisper.

"Too risky," Cody replied. "Let's try a window." He peered around the back of the house. Light spilled from what he remembered was Brady's study. Even better, one of the three windows was open. "Follow me and stay beneath the light from the windows," he instructed.

Once more in a crouch, Cody pushed around the house. Speed was of the essence. If the two guards outside the barns were alert, it'd be only minutes before one of them noticed their counterparts at the house were missing. And even if they weren't alert, moonrise was only about twenty minutes away. Once the moon's light bathed the prairie, the men were certain to notice the missing guards.

Cody slipped beneath the three lit study windows, then held up a hand to halt the lawman behind him. Turning, he pressed a finger to his lips. Patterson nodded. Cautiously Cody rose enough to peer into the closest window. Luck still rode on his shoulder. Not only was the middle window open, but Calvin Brady sat at his desk just a couple of feet in front of it. The senator's back was to the open window as he enjoyed a cigar and a glass filled with three fingers of what appeared to be bourbon.

With a glance around to make certain he went unseen, Cody crept beneath the open window, then stood up. He thrust the barrel of his rifle inside, pressing it to the back of Brady's neck.

"Make a sound or a sudden move and I'll blow your head off, Senator," he warned in a soft voice.

Brady stiffly nodded.

Cody kept the rifle barrel firmly against the senator's neck as he signaled Patterson to climb through the window. When the sheriff was standing in front of the desk with his own rifle leveled at Brady's chest, Cody slipped inside.

To his surprise, rather than fear darkening Brady's face, the politician smiled with amusement as he eyed the two intruders.

"I'd heard Major Jones hired only the best. But I didn't realize just how good his Rangers were until now. My boys should've run you down by noon." Brady chuckled. "Do you realize you got past four of my best men to reach this house?"

While Cody kept Brady covered, Patterson stepped to the study door and pressed an ear against it. "There's at least one man standing guard outside."

"And six others in the house as well as my sons," Brady said, his amusement growing. His eyes actually flashed with delight. "And every one of them is armed to the teeth. Seems like you two just jumped out of the frying pan and into the fire."

"Could be," Cody agreed as he walked around the desk and motioned for the senator to stand. "But if so, you're in the flames with us. If there's any burning, one of us will see that you get your share. I promise you that, Brady."

For an instant a shadow of a doubt crossed the senator's face. As quickly as it came it vanished, and the amused smile returned. "Perhaps. I guess we'll just have to wait and see."

"What I want to see is you over at that door, opening it very slowly and carefully," Cody ordered, prodding the man's stomach with the rifle barrel and directing him across the study. "Then tell your man to bring Charity Quitman in here. Tell him you want to question her."

Brady didn't hesitate. He opened the door, while Cody and Patterson stepped out of sight. "Lee, get the girl and bring her here. I've got a few more questions for her."

"Right, Senator," a voice out in the hall answered, followed by retreating footfalls.

Pressing the door shut before his captive decided to risk a cry for help, the Ranger returned Brady to his chair behind the desk. On top of the desk was the note Cody had watched the telegrapher write the evening before, when his message had arrived from headquarters.

Brady chuckled when he caught Cody's gaze, and he held up the note toward Cody. "You know, you really are something else, Cody. I doubt there's another lawman in this state who'd have thought of checking the reservations my wife made on the riverboat, the stage, and the train and made the connection between those three unrelated conveyances. But you—you jumped right on it. Amazing work!"

"Fifty-one men and women murdered to make certain your wife didn't divorce you, Senator," Cody said in a voice filled with contempt.

"Yes, but consider my dilemma. Piecing together the fact that Mary was heading for Fargo to divorce me was rather simple. But having to choose which of the three modes of travel she'd actually be on . . . well, that was an insurmountable problem. I had to see that all were stopped."

"You whoreson," Patterson growled. "That confession will cost you your life, Brady."

Brady chuckled again. "Confessions are useless, Sheriff, if they're not employed during a trial. And I will never be tried for my wife's murder, so my confession won't do you any good. You see, my men won't let you step one foot off this ranch alive. They have orders to shoot you down on sight. I've told them that you two and Miss Quitman are assassins come to kill me. Gentlemen, the loyalty of my men is beyond reproach. They will do as I say.''

''Like Jeff Shiner?'' An angry red tinged Patterson's face.

''Exactly like Jeff Shiner.'' Brady leaned back in his chair. ''Although in Jeff's case there was an added incentive of five thousand dollars to see that the Texas and Pacific train was wrecked and that Mary—if she was, indeed, actually on the train—died in the accident.'' He smiled with satisfaction. ''The fact that Mary hadn't been spotted anywhere near Jefferson seemed to rule out the riverboat. But, of course, I couldn't be too careful. The fellow who planted the explosive also helped with the rescue effort. He was to carefully check all the women survivors and make sure that if Mary had been on the boat and lived through the sinking, she never made it back to town.'' Brady shrugged. ''The stagecoach was a simpler matter, of course. There were only two women passengers, so the expedient thing to do was kill them both, just in case.''

Patterson started for the senator with the butt of his rifle upraised, but Cody grabbed him before he could take two steps. ''Someone's coming.''

The sheriff's head whipped around, cocking to one side as he listened. ''I'll handle the door,'' he said.

Patterson backed up against the wall next to the hinged side of the door; Cody edged around the desk and pressed the rifle barrel to the back of Brady's neck.

''Senator, I got the girl,'' a man's voice announced over a light knock on the door.

''Tell him to bring her in,'' Cody directed Brady.

''Let her in, Lee,'' Brady called, doing as he was told.

The door opened inward. Cody's pulse raced at the sight of Charity. She appeared unharmed as she stepped over the threshold into the study. Behind her came the man the senator had called Lee. He was completely inside the room before he noticed the Ranger holding the Sharps to Brady's head. Lee's hand darted for a holstered pistol.

Howard Patterson stepped forward. While his booted foot closed the door, his upraised arms drove the wooden stock of his rifle into the back of the cowhand's head. The man groaned under the impact, swayed unsteadily to the right, then collapsed in a heap on the floor.

"Cody!" Charity gasped. She darted across the study to hug Cody tightly and kiss him.

"There'll be time for sparkin' when we get out of here," Patterson said. "I suggest we put our minds to doin' just that."

Cody nodded. "Out the window and stay low," he directed Charity, then motioned Patterson outside after her. When the sheriff was in place on the other side with his rifle at the ready, Cody sent Senator Brady through the window and then climbed out after him. "Which barn holds your horses?" he asked Brady.

"The one to the right."

Charity touched Cody's arm. "He's lying. I could see the barns from the room they kept me in. The horses are stabled in the barn by the bunkhouse."

"That's the first stupid thing you've tried," Cody said angrily, jabbing the rifle barrel into Brady's back as he moved his prisoner toward the barn Charity had indicated.

A moon rising to the east cast its frosty light over the ranch as they walked toward the barn. While he, Charity, and Patterson stayed in the shadow, Cody kept Brady's face bathed in moonlight so that the single guard at the barn never suspected anything as the group approached. The first indication the man had that something was askew was when the butt of Cody's Sharps slammed into his chin. Then it was too late. The guard crumpled to the ground, unconscious.

Patterson stepped over the ranch hand, lifted the two-by-four that barred the double doors, and pulled one door slightly open. Cody gave Brady another jab with the rifle and followed him inside. Charity and Patterson were two steps behind him. Patterson found and lit a lamp hung on the wall near the tack room, providing the light he and Charity needed to saddle and bridle four mounts.

Patterson led two mounts toward the front of the barn. Charity came behind him with two other horses. "Keep an eye on him, and I'll get the doors," Cody said.

While the sheriff raised his rifle and leveled it at the senator, Cody shoved both doors wide. He froze. Six men stood outside, including Pete and George Brady, the senator's sons. All had revolvers in their hands.

"It's over," Pete said. "You've gone as far as you're going to go. Throw down your guns, and hike your hands."

"It's not over yet. Howard, show them what I mean," Cody called to the sheriff.

Behind him the lawman said, "In case the light's too dim for all of you to see good, I've got this Sharps pressed upside Brady's head. Any one of you makes a move I don't like, the senator'll die."

The six men shifted their attention from Cody to the interior of the barn. Cody could read the uncertainty on their faces.

"Move back and let us by," the Ranger ordered. "And don't even think about trying to follow us, because if we see one gun between here and Fort Worth, that Sharps is liable to go off."

Brady's sons and the four ranch hands backstepped.

"Okay, bring the horses out," Cody said to his companions. "We've overstayed our visit."

But Brady's voice shattered the calm. "I didn't raise my sons to be frightened women! I taught you to fight for what's yours! Goddammit, I told you to shoot these two on sight— and that's what I meant! Kill them! Do it now!"

Pete started to bring his pistol up.

"Damn!" Cody spat. He swung the Sharps around as he realized that his bluff had fallen through. His finger squeezed the rifle's trigger, and it exploded. Yellow and blue flame leapt from the barrel as it spat lead.

The older of Brady's sons died when a bullet tore into his chest. But the men beside him were quite alive. All of them raised their weapons.

There was nothing to do except ignore the screaming slugs that filled the air. Letting his reflexes rather than his brain control him, Cody jerked the Sharps toward the men and opened up. Behind him he heard the bark of Patterson's rifle.

Two of the cowhands doubled over and dropped. Pointing

his weapon rather than aiming, Cody continued to fire. A white-hot brand of pain lanced his left arm. Still he cocked cartridges into the chamber and squeezed off round after round down the line of three surviving men.

Whether it was his bullets or Patterson's that found their targets Cody didn't know or care. Each of the men facing him jerked spasmodically in death, then fell to the ground, their guns silenced.

The roar of the gun battle still filled his ears as he stared at the crumpled forms of the six dead men. He lived. Somehow he had survived the hail of bullets. Pain pulsed from his fingers to shoulder, and he pulled his gaze to his left arm. Blood, black in the moonlight, soaked the forearm of his shirt. It hardly mattered. He was alive.

"Howard's hurt," he heard Charity say behind him.

Cody turned. The sheriff stood weakly, supported by Charity. A dark stain spread across Patterson's right thigh. He looked up at the Ranger, gritting his teeth, and said, "It burns like hellfire, but it ain't a killin' wound. The bullet went clean through. I can ride. Help me into the saddle, and I'll ride out of here on my own."

Cody took a step toward the lawman, then halted. A crumpled mass lay on the ground near Patterson. It was Brady; he was dead. Cody eyed the sheriff.

"It weren't me, though God knows I wanted to put a bullet in him," Patterson said. "It was one of his own men that got him."

Cody looked back at the senator. Brady had said he'd never stand trial—and he had made certain that he wouldn't. He had known he stood in the line of fire. The choice had been his. He had cheated the hangman, but not death.

"You're bleeding!"

Cody pulled his gaze from Brady. Charity was pointing at his left arm. He shook his head. "It's not bad, a graze. We'll tend it as soon—"

A gasp came from Charity's throat. The crunch of stone beneath boots spun Cody around. The Cross B's hands came running from the bunkhouse, stopping before the barn with pistols and rifles in hand. Their glances darted between the dead and the threesome still standing. The moonlight was more than bright enough for Cody to read their expressions. They wanted blood.

"It's over," Patterson called while Charity kept him on his feet. "I'm Sheriff Howard Patterson from Terrell. This man"—he pointed to Brady—"was wanted for murdering his wife. He wrecked a train, blew up a riverboat, and had two women on a stagecoach killed to do that. Fifty-two men and women butchered in all."

A murmur ran through the cowhands. They listened, Cody thought, but they weren't convinced. Their guns remained raised and ready.

"My name's Cody," he told them. "I'm a Texas Ranger. Sent from San Antonio to investigate the train wreck Mary Brady was killed in—the same wreck Senator Brady admitted to arranging. Calvin Brady has paid for his crimes with his life. He died the way he lived, using people for his own ends." Cody nodded at the six dead men at the ranch hands' feet. "These men died with him—but it wasn't their fight any more than it's yours."

He paused, studying the cowhands. Their guns remained at the ready.

"Now the choice is yours," Cody continued. "You can cut us down, and we'll take some of you with us." He lied. His Sharps was empty, and there was no way he'd be able to draw the Colt before the cowboys riddled his body with bullets. "But where's the sense in that? What use is there in fighting for a dead man? Sheriff Patterson said it all. It's over."

For several uneasy moments the ranch hands stared at Cody and then at one another. One by one they lowered their weapons and drifted away, returning to the bunkhouse.

Cody let out a breath he hadn't even been aware of holding. He turned back to Charity and Patterson. "Let's get out of here before they change their minds."

CHAPTER

||||||||||||||||||||||||||||||||||| **19** |||||||||||||||||||||||||||||||||||

Cody left the Fort Worth telegraph office feeling that at last he had concluded the Texas and Pacific investigation. True, he still had to send his official report to Major Jones, but he'd handle that after a brief stop in Jefferson to meet with Manly Howell. Cody's wire to Howell had led to the arrest of one of the *Big Cypress Runner*'s crewmen, who admitted that Senator Calvin Brady had paid him two thousand dollars to place a keg of blasting powder next to the riverboat's boiler.

"Paper, mister?" a boy hawking newspapers called to Cody as he started to cross the street for the railroad station. "Read about Senator Brady! Only two cents!"

Cody handed over the money for a paper, then shot to the other side of the street, gingerly weaving between two horse-drawn wagons, and walked to the train platform. He pulled out his pocket watch, which read a quarter to three—fifteen minutes until the train pulled out, and Charity was nowhere to be seen. He frowned. She had promised to be here to say good-bye. Had Howard Patterson run into problems at the doctor's office?

Cody let out a breath. The sheriff was lucky to be alive. After the shoot-out at Brady's ranch, they had decided heading back to Cross Bee was too risky, so instead they rode for Fort Worth—a three-day journey that had nearly cost Patterson his life from loss of blood. He looked like a man with one foot and one hand in the grave when they finally reached a Fort Worth physician.

That had been two days earlier. When Cody had visited Patterson in his hotel room this morning, he appeared to be a man well on his way to recovery.

"First call for Dallas and all points east," a conductor shouted as he stood beside one of the train's two passenger cars and began to punch tickets.

Cody scanned the platform again. Still no Charity. What could be keeping her?

He shook his head and opened the newspaper he had just purchased. The front page was devoted to Calvin Brady and his crimes. Quickly perusing the story's multiple columns, Cody read the highlights. He smiled. The reporter's article attributed the uncovering of Brady's bloody deeds to East Texas sheriffs Howard Patterson and Manly Howell, working in conjunction with an unnamed Texas Ranger. Cody was pleased that his name hadn't made it into print. He much preferred anonymity.

For the most part the story was an accurate account of the investigation and the eventual confrontation with Brady and his men. However, the prose did take on a purple tinge when the writer got around to the gun battle on the Cross B. In print it took several minutes to read. Cody's memory of the shootout was fuzzy. He found it difficult to remember details, it had begun and ended so fast.

"Cody!"

He stuffed the paper into a pocket and turned to see Charity come running up the steps to the platform. She gasped for breath when she reached his side. "I was afraid I had missed you."

"We've only a few minutes until the train pulls out," he said. "How's Howard?"

"The doctor wants him to stay in bed and rest another three or four days. After that he'll be fit enough for a train ride back to Terrell. I'll stay here with him until then," she answered.

He didn't really want to discuss the sheriff's physical condition. What he wanted was to take this beautiful woman into his arms, hug her tightly, and kiss her—which he did.

She returned all the passion of his embrace, then gazed up

at him when they parted. "It's been a long time since I've been kissed like that," she murmured. "I've missed it."

"All aboard," the conductor called out. "All aboard!"

Cody wasn't certain how to respond. If time permitted he would've been happy to find out just where their kisses might lead. But there *was* no time; Ranger business called him.

"Are you certain you have to go?" she whispered, the question holding an unspoken plea for him to stay with her.

"Yes. I've an unfinished case back in San Antonio. After that's wrapped up, Captain Vickery'll be wanting me back in Del Rio." He kissed her again. "I'm a Ranger, Charity. That's my job."

"All aboard!" the conductor called out again.

Charity sighed. "I guess all I can hope is that you might visit Terrell again someday."

Cody smiled. "I just might do that." He didn't lie, though he realized the likelihood was small. The border country ranging from San Antonio to El Paso was his territory. Still, he could never tell. "I just might do that," he repeated.

With a final, hasty kiss, Cody released Charity, then turned and trotted toward the waiting conductor, who punched his ticket and waved him onto the train. He barely had time to find his way to a vacant pair of seats before the train jerked to life and began pulling away. Outside, Charity waved to him. Scooting next to the window, he watched her until she disappeared from view.

He smiled wistfully as he settled back in his seat. He actually regretted seeing this case come to a close—though it wasn't the end of the case he regretted, it was leaving Charity Quitman. Their kisses held unfulfilled promises. A man couldn't help but regret that.

Pulling the newspaper from his coat pocket, Cody opened it. He passed over the front-page story; he had had enough of Calvin Brady to last a lifetime. Like yesterday's news, Texas would soon forget Brady ever existed.

He turned the page and glanced over the headlines. A Jefferson dateline caught his eye. The story was an account of the U.S. Army Corps of Engineers using a new explosive called dynamite to clear the centuries-old logjam on the Red River. Apparently this dynamite was succeeding where scores of earlier efforts had failed. An Army spokesman was quoted as saying he expected the logs to be cleared within a month.

Cody quickly reread the article, making certain he hadn't misinterpreted the story. He hadn't. After hundreds of years, the waters of the Red River were expected to return to their natural course within a month.

He shook his head in disbelief. Jay Gould's three words scrawled in that hotel guest book flashed in his memory: JEFFERSON IS DEAD. Texas's largest city would be destroyed economically without riverboat trade on the Big Cypress. In a month Gould's prophesy—or curse—would come true.

"Dallas! Our next stop is Dallas," the conductor called as he walked through the passenger car.

Cody glanced out a window, staring at the small town built near the banks of the Trinity River—a river too narrow and shallow for a riverboat to travel. The cluster of homes and stores appeared out of place there in the middle of the prairie. He couldn't imagine why anyone would settle here and attempt to build a town, when the booming cattle town of Fort Worth was only thirty-five miles away. He wondered if maybe cities and towns were like the lives of men—one died and another was born. And Jefferson would die a quick death as the Big Cypress's water level dropped.

Cody studied the hamlet of Dallas for a few more seconds. *Who knows,* he thought idly, *even a nowhere town like this one might take Jefferson's place.*

He returned to his newspaper.